AFTERIMAGE

AFTER IMAGE

NAOMI HUGHES

PAGE STREET
PUBLISHING CO.

First published in 2018 by
Page Street Publishing Co.
27 Congress Street, Suite 105
Salem, MA 01970
www.pagestreetpublishing.com

Distributed by Macmillan, sales in Canada by The Canadian Manda Group.

22   21   20   19   18   1   2   3   4   5

ISBN-13: 978-1-62414-597-1
ISBN-10: 1-62414-597-3

Library of Congress Control Number: 2018932855

Cover and book design by Rosie Stewart for Page Street Publishing Co.
Author photo by Rebecca Kuehn, KRK Studios
Photograph of girl © Shutterstock / vgstudio; photograph of city
© Shutterstock / studioalef

Printed and bound in the United States

For everyone who's ever had to be brave.

CHAPTER ONE

FIFTEEN MINUTES BEFORE THE EXPLOSION, I'm trying to work up the courage to walk through a parking lot gate.

I used to love gates. There's something about the sleek straight lines, the bland iron of the bars, the honest minimalism of the decorative spikes that's always made me feel at home no matter where we were deployed. This gate, though, comes with a new feature: judgmental stares from the guards in the booth, along with muttered complaints from everyone who's driven past during the last twenty minutes while I failed to finish this morning's therapeutic homework.

Shame curls in my belly. I grit my teeth and keep pacing.

Fear weighs down my steps and tries to glue me in place; moving, even if it isn't in the right direction, is an act of defiance. I hate that it's the best I can do.

"Remember your diaphragmatic breathing," emanates a voice from my palm. I lift my phone. On the videochat app, Mom gives me a thumbs up. I grimace and return the gesture with as much enthusiasm as I can muster, which isn't very much at all, as massive panic attacks are emotionally-limiting douchebags that way.

Another car pulls up in the entry behind me and honks and I step to the side so it can go through. The man inside grumbles in my direction as his car slips past. I catch something about the "nuthouse" and my place therein.

The insult bites deep, but I give him a smile and a cheerful flipoff. Then one of the guards presses a button and the gate slides open and, for a moment, I hate nothing in the world more than the man in that car—not because he's a jerk, but because he can drive inside the agency base crowded with soldiers and scientists and too-close buildings without so much as a second thought.

I try to hang on to the anger—anything is better than this panicky suffocation—but it fizzles away in seconds like a defective Fourth-of-July sparkler.

I stop pacing. "Maybe we should just try this tomorrow."

"Breathe, Camryn," Mom repeats serenely.

"I *am* breathing," I argue.

"No, you're hyperventilating."

"Hyperventilation is a type of breathing."

She gives me a look. She approves of humor as a coping technique, but not as a defensive one. The biggest reason I both love and hate that my mom is also a psychiatrist: she knows all my bullshit, and buys exactly zero of it. A part of me is glad she's not my therapist. That title is reserved for a sweet grandmotherly doctor downtown, who also doesn't buy my bullshit, but at least must use more than a look to call me out on it. Mom just fills the role of support person— she talks me through my panic, keeps me grounded, and reminds me how unlikely it is that my therapy homework will actually kill me.

Not that I ever quite believe her.

I pace a few steps farther, stop in front of our ancient Toyota that's parked to the side of the entryway, and drop my forehead down to its hood. "I can't do this," I mutter into the chipped beige paint. The truth of the words scrapes my throat raw.

Mom hears it. Her eyebrows draw together. "Are you sure, baby?" she asks gently.

I listen for the disappointment in her voice, but it's not there. It's never been there. Not when I, the daughter of the agency's top psychiatric researcher, was diagnosed with panic disorder last year. Not when I had to switch to homes-chooling last month because I couldn't handle all the triggers at my public school. And not now, when I can't even manage to drive into the base to pick her up the morning after her exhausting double shift. She's got bags under her eyes and her gray-and-blue uniform is rumpled from the unusually long night of data analysis, but she hasn't complained once in the twenty minutes she's been coaching me through my latest failed attempt at overcoming my fear of fear. If I want any shot at going to college next year, I have to be able to function with anxiety, and she's determined to show me that's possible.

I drag myself upright. If she says I can do this, then I can do this. Panic disorder can shove it.

Easier said than done, though. I only manage to get ten feet from the gate this time before my hands start shaking, barely close enough to read *Fort Wells Army Base, Agency for Scientific Advancement Division* etched into the top bar. Beyond those bars looms the base, a vast spread of buildings belonging to the agency—a newly-created sector of the US Army dedicated to generating new technologies and research. Some they patent and sell to keep themselves funded, some they classify and integrate into the nation's defenses, and some, like Mom's research, they use to improve the Army's operations and procedures. Mom comes here every day along with thousands of her coworkers to do vital work for our whole country. The least I can do is manage to get through the gates.

I inch closer, trying to get near enough to touch the iron. That's part of my homework. Touch it, drive through it, then walk to Mom's office on the south end of the base. Baby steps, my therapist calls it. But I had a horrific panic attack when Mom brought me here a few months back, and after that I knew I was doomed to have another the second I set foot past this gate again. So, of course, that fear ended up actually causing the attack itself, and thus the list of places I can go without suffering crushing terror shrank that much more. Panic disorder: a self-fulfilling prophecy of suck.

A red car honks loudly behind me. I ignore it, forcing my foot to move just a few inches closer to the gate. My heart rate picks up. A sense of impending doom winds itself tight around my throat, choking off my air supply. I stop and wait.

These are symptoms of anxiety. They're not dangerous. I'm not going to die, not going to faint, not going to float away from myself like a clipped balloon. I'm *fine*.

Tears prick at my eyes and I force them back. I've already embarrassed myself enough today, damn it. I lift my phone. "How about meeting me in the parking lot?" I say, trying for a light tone like I don't care either way, but Mom doesn't answer. I glance down. White letters are blinking across the screen—*call dropped*. I have no data signal, not even enough regular signal to make a good, old-fashioned call. The local tower must be down. I groan and thumb the phone off, and the black screen reflects my features: tired brown eyes, set jaw, a pale face framed by short, choppy brown hair. I drop the useless phone into my pocket.

Off to the side, one of the guards in the booth straightens up, holding his own cell phone in one hand and muttering into a walkie-talkie in the other. He and his partner exchange a glance, and then he steps out onto the sidewalk to survey the street with one hand on his gun.

"Everything okay?" I call cautiously.

"Need to ask you to move along now, Miss Kingfisher," is all he says, eyes still on the cars.

Now or never. I take a deep breath and turn back to the gate. I curl my shaking hands into fists. It takes me a few minutes, but I finally manage to raise my arm. My fingers graze the frosty metal.

And then I wake up coated in ash.

———

I stay awake for the span of five heartbeats.

One. I'm lying in a fountain. Cracked, empty. Ash is everywhere. It coats the sky, lies thick across the fountain's rim, dulls my skin to an ugly pallor. It cakes on my tongue, dry and bitter, like I'll never taste anything else ever again. I inhale and choke on it.

Two. A gray sunrise. It's too high in the sky; I've lost time somehow. How much? Half an hour? My brain is fuzzed over, the panic numb and slow and confused. My heart stutters and trips like it's trying to restart, and then—*three.* I turn my head.

Skeletons of smoking framework clawing at the sky. Giant chunks of uprooted pavement looming overhead. A twisted iron bar speared into the concrete inches from my shoulder, tiny gray flakes gathering in the corners of its etched words: *...ntific Advancement Division.*

I breathe. The silence breathes. There's nothing but rubble. Soot. Ash. Silence.

Four. Except there is something else. Some*one* else. A boy is sitting at the edge of my fountain, knees drawn up, staring into the dawn like it's impossible to look at anything else. There's no ash in his blond hair, no gray smears on his stark-white lab coat, no smudges on his glasses. His eyes are green and bright like cut glass and the look on his face is *wrong,* terribly and deeply wrong, and if he looks at me with those eyes and that expression it will make whatever this is real and that can't happen, I can't let it. I flinch away. My arm knocks against the iron bar.

"There's a dead man at my feet," he says, not looking away from the sun.

I go still.

"You can't see him from there," he continues. "But he's burnt to a crisp. And I keep trying to take off my coat, I keep trying to cover him, but I can't. Because I think I might be dead too."

And then he turns and looks at me, and those awful, beautiful eyes pin me in place, and that's when I see that his lab coat is foggy around the edges and his torso is transparent and I can just make out the blackened wreckage of my mother's office building through his left shoulder.

"Tell me you can see me," he whispers.

Five.

I throw up. And then I pass out.

CHAPTER TWO

DREAM.

In my dream, there's an ambulance or maybe a helicopter. Red lights. Blue lights. Screaming. I don't know what the words are, but I'm the one screaming them and the boy's gaze is locked on mine like he has them all memorized, like they're part of a script he knows by heart.

"I can't remember my name," he says quietly. I stop screaming.

The paramedics who were fluttering around me like sugar-drunk hummingbirds slow. They eye each other with relief. Someone sticks a needle in my arm. Off to the side, a monitor beeps out a frantic rhythm.

"…blast radius… the only survivor," says one of the doctors, and everyone freezes.

I inhale. The scream rises in my throat again, and it tastes like ash.

"I think it might have something to do with the number five, though," the boy says quickly. "That was the first thing I thought about when I—when I came to a few minutes ago." His voice cracks a little, but he sets his mouth in a determined line.

My eyes flit back to him. The scream subsides into a cough, and someone claps a respirator over my mouth.

A dim thought struggles to the surface like a fish in murky water: they should've done that first. Dad would have their heads if they worked at his hospital.

"So maybe just call me Quint for now," the boy finishes, and gives me a half-smile. It's not really a smile, though. It's an anchor. I cling to it for all I'm worth, because: blast radius. Only survivor. The wreckage of my mother's office, the letters on the iron bar.

Oh God. Oh, my God.

The dream ends.

CHAPTER
THREE

WAKE UP COVERED BY a white sheet. It's too soft, too close to my face, and I feel like I'm drowning. When I try to drag it away my hands only twitch in response.

I blink, trying to clear my vision and restart my sluggish brain. The air tastes strange, metallic. Something is pinching the skin inside my elbow. Something else is beeping in a pattern that feels like it should be familiar. Groggily, my brain connects the dots:

Heart monitor. IV. Antiseptic.

Hospital.

Which means there should be a call button…somewhere?

I lift my head. The room is empty, but there's a TV in the corner and images blink over the screen—news anchors with grave faces, streets plastered in canary-yellow caution tape, an Army fence stabbed through rows of wilted flowers.

I stop scanning the room and squint at it, trying to make sense of the pictures. In the back of my mind something stirs. I shouldn't watch this. I should go back to sleep. I can't remember why, and I don't think I want to.

The shot changes to show President Vasquez. She clears her throat, folds her hands, gives a speech about *regrettable accidents* and *malfunctioning equipment* and how the agency is under investigation. Five thousand people dead, she says. Our nation mourns.

My heart monitor beeps. I stare at the TV, no longer caring that my eyes still won't focus right. *Our nation mourns.* That's what they say when there's some big tragedy, a plane crash or a school bombing or a sniper gone rogue. *Our nation mourns* means a week of that strange sadness that sort of belongs to you and sort of belongs to everyone, and then the flags go back up to full mast and the world rights itself again. That, I used to think, was mourning.

I was wrong. Mourning is the truth curled tight around the edges of your mind, and you huddle in the dark trying not to look.

I'm getting closer to being fully awake and I'm now very sure I don't want to be, so I take a shuddering breath and stretch out my fingers. They creep over the sheets toward the remote at my knee.

The TV blinks to another shot. It's from the stadium during some minor league team's practice. A player is grinning at the small early-morning crowd as he swings. A *crack* snaps across the field when he connects. People cheer—

And then a flash like a supernova. A second later, the sonic boom pounds into the camera and the picture shivers, goes fuzzy. When it comes back a mushroom cloud has bloomed over the top of the stadium wall.

The explosion. The ash, the wreckage, the end of my world.

Desperate now, I twist my fingers in the sheet and pull it up my body. The remote rides along with the fabric. When it's almost within reach I grab for it, but my hands are trembling and I accidentally knock it to the floor.

I spit out a shaky litany of every curse word my big brother ever taught me and dive after it, but I overcompensate and hit the ground like a sack of potatoes. The remote bounces off my IV line and skitters under the bed. I drag myself after it.

It's cool and dark here. The sheet hangs over the edge of the bed, a veil that narrows the world to me and the remote in the corner and the cool tile that smells a little bit like orange Lysol, which is exactly the brand Mom used to mop the floors of our apartment. I hate it. It always makes my throat ache.

I close my eyes and inhale.

Outside my sanctuary, someone clears his throat.

My eyes snap open. There's a boy on the other side of the sheet, sitting cross-legged on the floor. In the inch-tall gap between the tile and the blanket is a sliver of see-through lab coat.

"In 1633 Galileo Galilei was tried by the Roman Inquisition for his advocacy of heliocentric theory," he says. "He claimed the earth revolved around the sun. He was persecuted for it most of his life."

I inhale again. The Lysol smell burns, but not as much now.

"That's the part everyone always wants to talk about. The revolutionary scientist and the people who wanted to shut him up." His voice is conversational, quiet, like we're chatting at a coffeehouse. On the other side of the sheet his shape is nothing but a shadowy smudge. "But me, I wonder about the other people. The ones trapped in the middle with their new truth. There's a type of person who, when their world changes that way, doesn't have the option of hiding from it even if they want to. The earth revolves around the sun. The world is round. Your mother is gone."

My heart stutters in shock. I reach out, curl my fingers in

the sheet, yank it down—and come face to face with Quint.

He's got his hands folded in his lap. He's tall, lean, maybe two years older than me. His glasses are black and sophisticated, but they're sitting slightly crooked, undermining his intensity with a lopsided sort of charm. His lab coat is blindingly white and has no identifying insignia. And when he raises those beautiful bright green eyes to meet mine, all I can see is rubble and soot.

I tear my gaze from his. I will not look at him. I will not speak to him. I am fine, fine, fine, and I am going back to sleep. It doesn't matter what he says.

"Because here's the thing," he goes on like he hasn't just ripped a hole in my universe, "you should've woken up two weeks ago."

I flinch. No way in hell has it been two weeks.

"Your injuries are healing fine. Your brain is fine. The doctors can't figure out why the miraculous sole survivor of Fort Wells won't wake up, but I know why. It's because you didn't want to. You still don't want to."

I lie down on the tile, curl up, squeeze my eyes shut and inhale orange Lysol and order myself to ignore him.

"But you don't have a choice either. This is the world now. You have to live in it." His voice softens. "Your dad needs you to live in it."

I squeeze my eyes closed more tightly and try to shut

the words out, but the meaning leaks through anyway. Dad. Dad must be desperate. He'll need me to be here for him, need me to stay awake, but I can't. I can't bear it. But now I can't help it either—Quint's words have woken me up, and now my brain is working, and I *remember*. Oh God, I remember, and it feels like the world is burning all over again.

"And also," Quint goes on, his voice a little lighter, "I seem to know all sorts of random crap about science, and I need you to help me figure out why."

I go still. The burning stops. A different sort of fire starts—something ugly. Something almost...angry, as if I were somehow still capable of any emotion other than emptiness after the end of my world. He needs me to help *him*? This speech, forcing me to wake up, forcing me to think about what I've lost, it's so I can help solve *his* problems?

He watches the thoughts play across my face. He lifts his hands, lets them drop again. "It turns out," he says softly, "you're the only one who can see me." The easy conversational tone is gone and he sounds suddenly younger, and a little bit afraid. In the back of my head a voice whispers that if he is somehow real, his problems might be as terrible as mine. I don't listen to it.

I lift my head. I turn and look at him and open my mouth—and then the door creaks. A pair of scrub-clad legs stop in front of my bed. "Good morning," says their owner, who must be my doctor.

Quint and I are still staring at each other. I break eye contact first and he makes a frustrated noise, but I ignore him. I climb back into bed. "Hello," I reply, because I can't bring myself to say *good morning* back like everything is fine and normal and I'm okay with chitchat. My voice comes out rusty, which feels somehow right.

"Glad to see you're awake. I'll have a nurse let your father know—he just stepped out a few minutes ago, I believe. How are you feeling?" He gives me a once-over, then purses his lips and leafs through a few pages on his clipboard. *Dr. Browning*, says his name tag, which also identifies him as an agent. Am I in a military hospital? Or did all the surviving agents in the city scatter to other posts when their workplace was destroyed?

I shy away from the thought, lie down, and start pulling my sheet up off the floor. "I'm having hallucinations," I reply flatly.

Quint is still sitting cross-legged below me. A muscle in his jaw tightens but he doesn't look up. "Please don't call me that," he says in a low voice.

I ignore him. It doesn't matter. None of it matters. If he's a figment of my imagination, then I've been changed in even more fundamental ways that I don't want to think about; and if he's a ghost, then I'm stuck with the wrong one.

The doctor raises an eyebrow and scribbles something on the clipboard. I fight with myself for a few seconds before

I give in to the faint pulse of curiosity. "What are you writing?" I ask. Thanks to having two doctor parents, I know all the diagnoses, all the reasons I might be hallucinating this boy—schizophrenia, PTSD, certain kinds of drugs—but none of them quite fit. Maybe the doctor knows what Quint is and how to make him go away.

But a strange expression crosses Dr. Browning's face and he steps back. "Sorry. Your medical records are part of an ongoing investigation into the explosion at the base. They're agency property—I can only share limited information with you."

"You can only share limited information with me about my own condition?"

He scribbles some more. "That's correct."

I pause. When he looks up, I nod politely like a docile little patient, answer a few more questions about how I'm feeling, and then, when he's distracted by a nurse who comes to check my IV, I steal the clipboard.

So maybe I do care. Or maybe I just don't trust people who won't give me straight answers.

"Hey!" The doctor turns, spots me, and snatches his clipboard back before I have time to do more than read my own name. He flips through, making sure I didn't steal anything, and then retreats like he's afraid I'll make another grab for it.

I lay back down and curl up on my pillow. It doesn't matter, I remind myself dully. It won't bring her back.

Quint regards me from the corner of the room, thoughtful.

I roll over and go back to sleep.

———

The next day, the protestors descend.

I'm hobbling down the sidewalk just outside the hospital. The air is cool and foggy. I've got my bathrobe on over my pajamas because I'm cold and also because putting on normal clothing felt too much like saying life is also back to normal. Quint drifts along behind me—he can never seem to get more than ten feet away. I don't feel a thing when he reaches the end of whatever it is that tethers us together, but if I move too fast he gets dragged along behind. Not that I've been doing much hurrying.

Every few yards we pass an agent. I ignore them. I ignore everyone. And that's why, when I get hit by the first rotten apple, my only thought is that someone must've accidentally dropped their breakfast.

And then the signs come out.

PRESIDENT VASQUEZ=LIAR IN CHIEF.

JUSTICE FOR FORT WELLS!

WE THE PEOPLE DEMAND A PUBLIC HEARING!

The protestors are lining the sidewalk, melting out of buildings and side streets. They're heading for the agents behind me, who are clustering into a group and looking alarmed, lifting their walkie-talkies. One of them puts his hand on his gun.

Someone shouts. A camera flashes. *Splat!* Another apple crashes near my feet, spraying brown rot on the hem of my hospital-issued bathrobe.

I stare down at it. I wonder, faintly, where they got it. Have they been squirreling away their fresh apples for the last two weeks, waiting for them to rot for just this occasion? Is there some sort of rotten apple warehouse where people can get last-minute protest fruit?

"You okay, honey?" says a woman's voice, cutting through the jeers of the protestors and the agents' shouting.

I look up. A stocky, matronly woman is watching me, one hand on my shoulder and the other on a cardboard sign. She glances down, takes in the hospital bracelet on my arm, the entourage of agents huddled a few yards behind me. Her gaze softens. "You're the sole survivor, aren't you? The one everyone's talking about."

The sole survivor. That's what everyone has been calling me, even though it's not technically true. Most of the northern half of the base survived along with the agents who were stationed there. But I was found in the south, near the epicenter. Everyone who was within a three-mile radius of me is dead.

"I'm sorry about what you've been through," the woman says, and there's a choked quality about her voice that I recognize all too well. I don't register it as grief quickly enough to move though, and I'm trapped in the line of fire for what she says next. "I lost my daughters in the accident. I can see you've lost someone too. I'm so sorry."

Too late, I take another step away. The grief roars up again, made fresh by her words, and I try to smother it before it can smother me.

Three agents swoop out of nowhere, push the woman away, and clear a path through the other protestors. They hustle me back to my room. Two guard the door and shout into their walkie-talkies while the last one helps me to my bed and fumbles with an explanation. Someone leaked info about a potential person of interest in the investigation and now people think the agency has been covering something up about the explosion. They've been cornering agents with flash protests all over the city, demanding more information. They're angry. They're grieving. Things could get ugly, and I should make sure not to speak to any of the protestors just in case. Did I say anything to any of them? Anything that could be misconstrued, anything that might've been classified?

Another agent wedges through the door and slams it behind him. Apparently some of the protestors followed him into the hospital and the agency is still separating them from the people who have a legitimate reason to be here. Did I see if there were any cameras? Could I identify who threw the fruit?

Everyone asks questions. No one brings me a new bathrobe.

I stand up. "Get out of my room. I am going back to sleep."

No one listens. I go to sleep anyway.

My therapist visits and convinces my doctors that a brief field trip might do me good. Dad comes. He prods me awake, brings me a change of clothes, takes me out for a picnic lunch. We eat peanut butter sandwiches by the ocean and pretend we're okay, but we're sitting too far away from each other and there's enough food for three people, not two.

The peanut butter sticks to my throat. Quint sits at my side, silent for now. Dad takes me back to the hospital.

I have a panic attack. I cry. I go back to sleep.

Things go on like that for a week. Reporters call, and I ignore them. A parade of agency doctors interrogate me about my symptoms and, when they refuse to answer my questions, I ignore them too. I keep the TV off. I eat in my room. I tell Dad he should go back to work. I sleep as frequently as the nurses and my therapist will allow.

Mom might've called it depression. I call it the world without her.

It's a lie that finally wakes me up.

The agent who tells it is tall, black, and allergic to bullshit. She also has a security clearance higher than God, judging from the bright red number on her agency ID. She blusters into my room in the middle of the night, trailing a wake of spluttering nurses whom she shoos away with a look, and grabs an ugly plastic chair from the corner of the room.

Dad's been spending every night in that seat. Even my prodigal brother Kyle spent a few hours there while I was asleep, or so I've been told. So when the agent snatches it up like it belongs to her and drags it to my bedside—letting it screech against the linoleum and probably waking every patient within five rooms of me—a twinge of aggravation makes my shoulders hunch. It fades quickly, though. Everything does now.

She turns the chair around, drops into it backwards, and folds her arms over the top. "So," she says without preamble, "you've got some balls."

I blink—and then narrow my eyes. The line sounded offhand but her gaze is too calculating, too watchful. She's trying to shock me. This is some kind of test.

I bare my teeth in a syrup-sweet smile. "Thanks," I reply. "You too." Whatever she's selling, I'm not buying. All I want to do is go back to sleep.

She lifts an eyebrow. Her face looks like it doesn't quite

know how to smile, but one corner of her mouth pulls up in something that could almost be mistaken for approval. She holds out a hand. "Dr. Lila. I'm one of the agency's directors."

She worked with Mom, then. She must've been off duty the day of the explosion. "What do you want?" I ask, ignoring her hand. My voice is rusty, and I hope she takes the hint to go away. Then again, she doesn't look like the hint-taking type.

She drops her hand. "You told one of your doctors you were seeing hallucinations."

In the corner of the room, Quint stirs.

I don't look up. I've gotten good at that.

"That was right before you tried to steal your own medical chart," Dr. Lila goes on. "Hence: balls. You do realize stealing classified information is a felony, right?"

"Then take me to jail," I reply flatly, and roll over so I'm facing the window. "How much worse could it be?"

"Your dad could be completely alone," she says, and suddenly the room seems too small and my blanket too heavy.

I swallow. I roll back over to face her. She waits a second to be sure she has my attention, then continues. "They're releasing you in a few minutes. Your dad is already in the waiting room. You could go home."

The *if* hangs in the air between us. I refuse to touch it.

Her almost-smile flattens the tiniest bit with something

like sympathy. It makes me hate her even more and also, against my will, like her a little.

I give in. "If I do what?"

"Assist the investigation. And your own treatment, for that matter. The more we know about what happened to you that day, the more likely we'll be to find a cure for your hallucination problem." She pulls a paper-thin tablet from her briefcase and powers it on.

Quint moves closer and the room's shadows slide through him. He steps around the end of the bed—he pretends he can't walk through solid objects, as if it comforts him to fake interactions with reality—and ducks his head, trying to catch my eye. "I keep trying to tell you, I don't need to be *cured*." His tone is low and hard, but his voice catches at the end, just the tiniest bit.

I look up. He blanks his expression out too late and I catch the glint of fear. Uneasy, I keep my eyes on him, but he looks away after a second. It's odd to see him shaken. I don't think I like it. And I don't like that I don't like it.

Dr. Lila is still busy with her tablet. "Let's get some history first. Your therapist and your mom were working with you on CBT therapy for your panic attacks, right? Does your history with that include hallucinations?"

My gaze snaps back to her. "It's panic *disorder*," I correct her. It's been a year since I was diagnosed and the words still leave a bitter taste in my mouth. "And it's an anxiety disorder. It has literally nothing to do with hallucinations."

She ignores me, leaning over her tablet to enter her passcode, tilting the screen away from me. "What does he look like?" she asks in an offhand tone, like it doesn't really matter.

I stare at her. Slowly, in the back of my mind, suspicion stirs.

"Miss Kingfisher?" she prods.

I narrow my eyes. When I speak, my voice is steady. "I never told anyone my hallucination was a he."

She raises her gaze. Whatever she's really feeling, it's shuttered away behind a façade of cool amusement. "You mentioned it in your sleep," she says, and her voice is just as steady as mine.

I sit back. We watch each other. The suspicion in the back of my mind shifts, spreads.

Quint is looking down at his hands, still tight on the bedrails. It takes him a moment to raise his eyes to mine, and when he does, I see that spark of fear one more time before he screws it down tight. He's afraid of what answer I'll give her. He's afraid of whose side I'll take. And what does it mean that my hallucination can be scared?

I make myself hold his gaze as I answer Dr. Lila. "He's pudgy," I tell her. I lay down the lies in a neat line like I'm building a wall: "Short. Buck teeth. Terrible hair and the worst case of acne you've ever seen. Also, I'm pretty sure he doesn't like you." That last one isn't a lie, at least.

Quint blinks. His hands loosen and drop away from the rail and he tilts his head. "Pudgy," he repeats after a second, and his eyes are still careful, but there's an almost indiscernible trace of laughter in his tone.

Dr. Lila's expression doesn't change. She thumbs the tablet off and drops it back into her bag. "Your lack of cooperation doesn't lead anywhere you want to go, Miss Kingfisher." She gets up, walks over to the window. Distant shouting filters through the glass from outside. In the bottom corner of the frame I catch a bright blue-and-red flash. The police have had at least four cars stationed at the hospital's main entrance all day, keeping the mob of protestors and conspiracy theorists at bay across the street—I'm guessing they decided to camp out here because it's a military hospital with plenty of agency higher-ups to harass.

Dr. Lila pulls back the curtain, revealing the protestors' signs. One at the front is filled with the crossed-out photos of half a dozen smiling young agents who must've died in the explosion. The woman holding it is the one I met a few days ago, the one who put her arm around me, the one who'd lost her daughters. My gaze goes to the photos again, trying to pick out which women have her curly hair or kind brown eyes.

Bile rises in my throat. I want to look away, but don't.

Dr. Lila waves a hand at them, motioning at the front row where protestors are yelling at the police and shaking their fists. "They know a rogue agent was responsible for the explosion," she says.

My breath stutters. I turn back to her, ice creeping through my veins. "The...the president said it was an accident."

"The president doesn't know what I know."

She dangles the bait and waits, and I'm helpless to do anything but swallow it whole, because of course, of *course*, I need to know. It's suddenly all that matters in the whole world: knowing why my mother died. I try to tell myself it doesn't matter, dead is dead...but *murdered*, that's so much worse, so much uglier than *died in an accident.* "What do you know?"

She glances at me over her shoulder, eyes cool. "That your mother was working late on an unknown project every night for a week before the explosion. That she had contact during that week with individuals at higher clearance levels who were also flagged as potential rogues."

I try to understand what she's saying, but the ice in my veins has crept into my brain too.

Dr. Lila glances back at the mob across the street. "That group out there, they're convinced someone is at fault. And now they're convinced you have something to do with that someone. Probably because I've been leaking intel that confirms it. As of this morning, everyone in the city knows there's a link between the sole survivor and our prime suspect. I only meant that you were a family member, of course, but naturally they assumed you'd been involved in the attack too." She flicks the curtain, lifts her chin at the mob. "You think those signs are bad? You should see their social media. They were out for blood before, but now they're downright vicious. It's a good thing they don't know your name. It's a good thing they don't know where you live."

She's still looking down at the crowd. The curly-haired woman has flipped around her sign, the one with all the crossed-out pictures of the dead. On the back is a blurry picture of me in my hospital robe. It's been slashed through with a bright red marker. Underneath it is scrawled *No refuge for murderers.*

They aren't camped out here because it's a military hospital. They're here for me.

I've seen protests before. I've seen hate rallies on TV, I've seen mobs get ugly. But this—this kind woman, who found time to encourage me when she was grieving the loss of her children, who is now screaming at the top of her lungs and shaking that picture of me at the cops in front of her—this, I can't process.

And then I turn back to Dr. Lila. I look at her poker face, at that one raised eyebrow, and I watch her watching me, waiting for my reaction...and the suspicion in the back of my mind flares into something full of embers and the beginnings of fury.

Dr. Lila is the reason that woman is carrying that sign. She leaked that intel just for this moment—so that when she threatened me, I'd know she meant it.

Anger makes my words sharp and hard. "Are you saying you'll dox me if I don't cooperate?"

That smile, that awful tiny sympathetic half-smile, is back. "It's my job to protect you, Camryn. For as long as you choose to be involved in my investigation."

The space between us goes blank and fuzzy, like static on a TV screen. Or maybe it's just me—because her words from earlier are finally penetrating. I was so shocked by what she'd said about me that I hadn't fully understood what she was saying about my mother.

She thinks the explosion wasn't an accident. She thinks my mother was involved. She wants me to rat on her, in exchange for protection from the seething mob outside, in exchange for not throwing me in prison.

Quint is still watching me, gaze intent and waiting, but I don't look at him. The rage is too bright, too hot, like a flash fire that goes on and on. I look Dr. Lila in the eye. Then, because there's no way in hell my mother is a murderer and because it feels so *good* to be anything other than sad and scared and tired, I lean in close and give her a confidential smile and whisper like I'm telling her a secret: "Screw you too, ma'am."

She could dox me. She could bring the mob down on me. She could tell the cops I stole classified intel and have me thrown in jail. But the thing is, when you threaten somebody *that* much in *that* short a span of time, it means you're desperate. It means she needs me and if she does any of those things then she'd lose her leverage, and without leverage she'll have lost her chance at getting whatever it is she needs so badly from me.

Her blackmail is a lie that tells the truth. It's the lie that wakes me up. Entirely by accident, she's revealed that she has everything to lose, and I have nothing.

It's a stalemate.

Someone bangs on the door behind us. Without taking her eyes off me, she calls, "What?"

"Sorry to interrupt, but the girl's father is in the waiting room demanding to be let in."

Dr. Lila's cool expression shifts into something more dangerous. She says to me, "You know what, I think I'll have a word with him before you're released." She slips out of the room as silent as a ghost.

As soon as she's gone, Quint says, "Her password is AR8H673R9."

I go still. Then, slowly, I turn. He's sitting on the bed next to me now, hands clasped loosely between his knees, giving me a look that blazes with challenge. Go ahead and keep ignoring me, it says. I dare you.

It takes a second for my brain to shift gears before I understand what's happening. He's talking about the tablet. The one that's still in the briefcase on the floor. He saw the password. When he was standing next to Dr. Lila and I couldn't even see the screen, he watched what she entered and remembered it, which means he can see things I can't. Which means...what?

My gaze falls to the tablet. It's sticking out of her bag, powered down and a hundred times more dangerous than stealing a flimsy medical record—but it could give me a hundred times more answers, too. And if Dr. Lila has enough influence to set a mob against me, do I really have any option other than to find out those answers before she makes her next move?

A little thought slips through the back of my mind, quiet as a whisper: I could find out what she knows. I could find out what happened to my mother.

I could find out if she's innocent.

I crack down hard on the if, drop it into the still-burning fury and watch it wither. My mother is innocent. I will prove it, to the agency and to myself.

Quint waits. I slide to the floor but keep my eyes on him as I pull out the tablet. When I slip it into my backpack, he smiles.

CHAPTER
FOUR

I HOLD MY BREATH WHEN Dr. Lila takes me to meet
Dad. Her briefcase dangles off her frame, heavy with
the weight of the laminated hospital menu I replaced
her tablet with. She'll know exactly who stole it the second
she spots that, but she would've figured it out quick enough
anyway. The best I can hope for is that she won't look in
her bag again till tomorrow morning, which would give me
the whole night to sift through whatever information the
agency is trying to hide from me.

If the password Quint gave me works.

Oh my God, what am I doing? Trusting the word of
a hallucination, that's what. My steps falter, but I grit my
teeth and shove the anxiety down. I have no idea if I'll

succeed and I'm terrified of what Dr. Lila might do to me after this, but she was already blackmailing me with a felony charge and mob violence. At least this way I might have some leverage of my own, and a shot at proving she's lying about Mom. Right?

Dad is waiting at the front desk. The sight breaks me out of my thoughts and I stop for a second and watch him, because even though I've seen him nearly every waking moment of the last week, I'm realizing now that I haven't truly looked at him once in all that time. His dark hair is sticking up in tufts and there are purple half-circles under his eyes. He's wearing his paramedic gear. One sleeve is splattered with what I'm willing to bet is double strength espresso, which means he was probably pulled off an on-call shift to pick me up. He always hits the hard stuff when he's stressed. And how could he not be?

A wave of guilt floods me. He needs me as much as I've needed him, and I haven't even taken the time to ask how he's doing.

He spots me. Relief washes over his features and he pulls me into a hug that smells like shaving cream and antiseptic. I breathe it in, relaxing in the safety and familiarity until my backpack drags at my shoulder, heavy with the weight of the government property I've just stolen. Stricken with guilt yet again, I step out of the hug a second before I really want to.

He holds me at arm's length. "So. That's what you wear to commit grand larceny? Allegedly," he adds with a frown aimed at Dr. Lila.

I freeze up, the backpack's strap burning on my shoulder—and then realize that Dr. Lila must've told him about last week's attempt at medical record thievery. Although apparently the news didn't quite have the effect she intended.

Her smile tightens a few degrees. On anyone else, it would look pained. On her, it looks...dangerous.

I glance down at my fluffy hospital bathrobe, which I've been wearing in several variations for the last eight days. At least this one doesn't have the rotten apple stain. "You know what they say. A comfy larcenist is...something."

"Unsuccessful?" Dad supplies.

"Touché."

"Thank God," he mutters, then hands me a bag full of fresh clothes to change into. He nods over my head at Dr. Lila. "Goodbye, ma'am. I hope to continue our discussion on interrogating minors without notifying their parents at a later date."

"I can hardly wait," she replies, managing to make it sound both cordial and threatening. Her gaze lingers on me a few seconds too long, and her smile—I hate that smile, because I understand it now. It says she feels sorry for me, but she'll do what she's gotta do anyway, and screw me if I get in the way.

When Dad turns his back, I flip her off. It doesn't make me feel any better.

Dad pulls me away. "Come on, larcenist," he says to me. "Go get changed. And then you're grounded."

———

My doctors give me warnings, instructions, and a massive sheaf of discharge paperwork. I'm to get plenty of rest, light exercise is okay, and also the new implants in my leg and shoulder might set off metal detectors. That last bit is news to me, but when the nurse asks if I have any questions, I shake my head. I just want out of this place as quickly as possible.

A posse of agents herds us out a secret side door to avoid the protestors. Dad and Quint and I get in the car—a new Honda, not the Toyota that must be a heap of charred metal in some city junkyard by now—and huddle back into our separate islands of silence. When we turn out of the parking structure, I get a glimpse of the mob. They have more signs but I turn away without reading them, the fury still boiling low in my belly. I don't want to think about it. I don't want to think about them.

We drive. We park. We walk.

Our apartment is full of three-week-old dirty dishes and scattered heaps of laundry. Judging by the nest of blankets and sci-fi novels on the couch, Dad's been sleeping there on the nights he hasn't spent at the hospital. He has managed to clear off the table, though, and apparently empty the trash.

He's also taken down all the pictures of Mom.

I stand in the entryway and stare at the spot on the wall where last year's family photo used to hang. The square that's left behind seems to glow in comparison to the darker beige wall around it, like a shadow in reverse. Like an afterimage: the ghost of light that's left behind when you've been staring at something too bright for too long. I try to decide whether this makes the emptiness in my chest more or less painful.

Dad closes the door behind us. "It wasn't your fault," he says, quietly enough that I can pretend not to have heard him. He rubs a tired hand across his eyes and sets the pharmacy bag he's been carrying down on the hallway table. It's full of the meds the hospital sent me home with, mostly refills for the anti-anxiety pills that sometimes help lessen the frequency and intensity of my panic attacks, though unfortunately they can't make me forget my fears or the fact that I'm responsible for my mother's death.

But I don't say anything about that to Dad, because I know what he'd tell me. It's the same thing everyone's been telling me. Mom's death was a direct consequence of whatever agency equipment malfunctioned three weeks ago and destroyed the entire southern half of the base, and I couldn't have predicted the future, and she wouldn't have wanted me to blame myself. None of that matters, though. If I had been able to act in spite of my anxiety, I'd have picked her up on time, and if I'd picked her up on time she'd still be alive, and this is the only thing that can be true, because according to Dr. Lila, the only other possibility is that my mother somehow meant for the explosion to happen.

Either it's my fault she's dead, or it's her fault she's dead. There is only one of those options that I can live with.

Quint is watching me like he can read my thoughts from the way I'm gritting my teeth—and maybe he can, I caved a few days ago and told my visiting psychiatrist and, incidentally, the ever-present Quint, that Mom's death was my fault—and I make an effort to smooth out my features before Dad reads them too and figures out something's wrong. I clear my throat and reach for the pharmacy bag. But when I scoop it off the table, something glimmering and metallic slides out from beneath it and falls to the floor with a musical tinkle.

A bracelet. Slender white-gold chain. A delicate feather etched on the centerpiece. The memory reaches out and swallows me up before I can stop it.

I'm handcuffed to a desk when Mom shows up.

Her lips thin out as she spots my arm, twisted awkwardly too far beneath me so the store manager could lock the other cuff securely around the leg of his fancy cherrywood executive desk. I give Mom a weak smile and try to pretend I wasn't crying three minutes ago, but her laser vision picks up the quiver in my expression and the tear tracks I tried to scrub away before she got here.

She turns her gaze on the manager. Her pretty pearl earrings—a gift from Dad this morning for their day-long anniversary date, which my arrest has interrupted—sway.

The manager crosses his arms. "I caught her shoplifting," he says, belligerent.

"And you had to cuff her to your desk? She's only thirteen." Mom's tone is cordial, but around her purse straps her fingers twitch like she's remembering her Army training and how she knows at least a couple dozen ways to kill a man.

"And this is worth a hundred dollars." The store manager stabs a finger at the bracelet on his desk. It's white gold, beautiful and delicate, everything I'm not but wish I was. What made me want it most of all was the feather engraved on its little metal plate. Mom and I used to go bird-watching together before she got deployed to this new and much bigger city. I miss watching the birds together, like I miss everything about our old home. I lingered over the feather bracelet for a few minutes longer than I should've when the saleslady got it out of the case for me to try on. It shouldn't have mattered, this little scrap of jewelry, but somehow all at once it had symbolized everything about my old life that I'd loved and lost. If I could just have this, maybe I'd feel okay again. But then I saw the way-too-expensive price tag and everything in the whole world was miserable and off, and I knew I would never be anything but the perpetually homesick new girl, and I had to get out of the store before I broke down and cried in front of the new friends I'd gone shopping with.

By then the saleslady had gotten distracted by a girl asking to look at a necklace, so I'd walked off, focusing so much energy on not crying that I hadn't even realized I was still wearing the bracelet.

"Uncuff her, please," Mom says. Her tone is still respectful and the manager puffs up a little. I might know Mom's a soldier, but all he sees is a soft-voiced woman with messy chestnut hair and her favorite pair of comfy mom jeans, which I told her last week she needed to donate to a charity.

This was supposed to be her day off. And instead of relaxing with Dad for their anniversary, she had to come pick up a kid who is now a criminal.

She reads my thoughts, reaches out and brushes her fingers across my cheek. When the manager's not looking, she winks at me.

I blink, not sure what she's doing, but give her another shaky smile anyway.

"I'm gonna need to fill out a police report first," the manager says, arms still crossed, a smug look on his face like handcuffing a terrified thirteen-year-old was the highlight of his year. "I'm sick of these spoiled kids getting away with all this crap. No way is she getting off with just a slap on the wrist if I have anything to say about it."

Mom's expression goes frosty. She leans over the desk, her movements precise and controlled, and her Army tattoo peeks out *from under the neck of her shirt. The manager's eyes cross as he spots it and his smug look evaporates. He tries to replace it with one of disgust, hiding his new uncertainty. "Fine," he says, tossing the cuff's key on the desk. "Get her out of my sight. And maybe learn some better parenting skills so your kid doesn't shoplift next time she spots something shiny." He busies himself digging in his desk drawers, probably so he doesn't have to look Mom in the eye again.*

Mom uncuffs me without a word, steers me out to the car, and pulls out of the parking lot.

"I'm sorry," I tell her when we turn onto the highway. "I swear I didn't try to steal it."

She grins suddenly, reaches into her jacket pocket, and tosses the bracelet into the cup holder between us. "Ain't no thing, kid."

I gape at her. "But...you..."

She flips on the blinker and then levels a finger at me. "Stealing is wrong," she says sternly. "Do as I say, not as I do." Then her grin reappears and she turns on the radio and whistles along, oblivious, and like the sun flashing out from behind a cloud for just a second, I see her: a fierce, beautiful, and completely foreign badass who is somehow wearing my mother's old mom jeans.

I shake myself out of the memory. Dad is staring at me, concerned, and I fake a smile that nobody believes as I sweep the bracelet up and drop it into my pocket. The memory leaves an aftertaste—the foreignness of my mother in that moment, the way she'd transformed into a stranger right in front of me. At the time it had been amazing, but now it turns my stomach.

Maybe I really didn't know her all that well.

I hitch my backpack higher, feeling the weight within, and that sick uncertainty hardens and flashes back to anger. It's Dr. Lila who's done this to me, Dr. Lila who planted this awful doubt in my head, Dr. Lila who's tried to steal all I have left of my mother. And now I can prove it. As soon as I can get Dad to leave me alone with the tablet.

I fake a yawn. "I think I'm gonna go to bed, if that's okay."

Dad blinks and nods, trying not to look disappointed. He probably wanted to hang out with me now that I'm finally home. Mentally, I kick myself—I am seriously the worst daughter ever, especially after he stood up for me at the hospital. It can't be helped, though. I'll hang out with him when I get this mess straightened out.

Dad walks me to my room. He stops at the threshold and holds up his fingers. "Three things," he tells me. "One: I love you. Two: please try to cooperate with the agency, at least for now. I'm hiring a lawyer to get access to your medical records, but we need to do things the legal way and not the way that's going to get you tossed in jail for the rest of your natural life. Three: I'm going to bed. If you plan to commit any more crimes, I implore you to wait at least eight hours."

I manage to scrape up a smile. "I love you too. And no promises."

He ruffles my chopped-off hair and then trudges toward the couch.

I close the door. I sit gently on the bed. I pull out the tablet.

I hit the button and it powers up to a bloodred background. PASSCODE, prompts the screen.

I bite my lip. Quint is standing on the other side of the room, pretending to study the *Doctor Strange* poster above my dresser, but I can feel the weight of his attention. As much as this moment belongs to me and my mom, it belongs to him too. Either this'll validate him as being—well, something—if he really did read the password when I couldn't even see the screen, or we're both screwed.

I enter the password. It works.

I swallow and cast a sideways glance at Quint. He lets out a breath, dropping his faux interest in the poster, and slides onto the bed. He scoots closer to read over my shoulder. If he were real, I'd be able to feel his warmth. I bite back the instinct to lean toward him, unsettled by the reaction.

Then I pull up the home screen and a sudden onslaught of anxiety buries me. My fingers hesitate above the on-screen keyboard. If I go looking through these files, I might find something I don't like. I might find something I can't stand.

But if I don't open the files, isn't that as good as admitting there's a chance, however small, that my mom really could be some kind of traitor?

I open the main menu.

A list of files cascades down the screen: session logs, special projects, medical records. I click on a medical file at random. If my luck holds, maybe it'll tell me what Quint is. But a dialog box pops up: *Sorry, this file is corrupted.* Behind the box, a stream of symbols and gibberish fills the document.

My chest tightens. I click on the next, then the next.

Corrupted, corrupted, corrupted. Every single one.

I drop the tablet on the bed like it's hot, scoot away, and stare. This isn't possible. How could her tablet be working fine one minute and then have all its data suddenly corrupted just half an hour later? Unless...they already know what I've done. Unless this is some kind of anti-theft measure.

My eyes burn and I cover them with a hand. This was all I knew to do. I have no plan B, and I can't go back to living half-asleep, not after this. Dad said he's hiring a lawyer and maybe we can sue to get all Mom's records too, which might give me answers, but there's got to be miles of red tape between us and it. Eventually we'll run out of money to pay the attorney, and in the meantime, there's no way Dr. Lila will let me out of her sight, much less leave sensitive documents where I can steal them again.

I'll never know for sure. I'll have to live with this awful churning uncertainty forever, trying to convince myself I know the truth about the people I love the most. And—I'll never find out what's really wrong with me now. I'll be stuck with this, this ghost or hallucination or whatever Quint is, and God knows the agency isn't going to tell me anything about him.

Chirp. I pull my hand away from my eyes and peer at my Captain America shield bedspread. My new phone is nestled just under the star, blinking with a text notification. I hesitate—I'm sick of the well-wishers and even more sick of the reporters—but pick up the phone anyway, because it could be Kyle. I've tried to get in touch with my big brother half a dozen times since I woke up but deleted every message I almost sent him. I want to talk to him, but even more, I want him to want to talk to me. That's the only thing that could make tonight even a tiny bit okay.

But it isn't Kyle. It's a message from an unknown number. *I know you stole the agency tablet,* it says. *I'll be at Fish N' Chips at midnight. Let's meet.*

I stare at it, my skin prickling, terror lodged in my throat. Possibilities flash through my mind at a hundred miles an hour.

It's Dr. Lila. She left the tablet on purpose and I've played right into her plan.

It's an ally. Another victim of the agency, someone who knows how to fix the tablet and access the data I need.

It's someone else, a third party who wants me to sell them the government secrets I tried to steal. Which might now include my mother's data along with my own medical records.

I glance at the time, my heart pounding in my ears, flushing my system with anxiety and adrenaline. Eleven thirty. If Dr. Lila isn't the one who texted, how long do I have before she figures out her tablet is gone and comes after me? I'm already risking prison. There aren't many ways it can get worse from here.

"Cam," calls Dad from down the hall, "do you want anything to eat before I crash?"

I hesitate. Last chance. I could ask him to make me some waffles, and he'd burn them and then I'd have to make them, and we'd eat them like sandwiches with ice cream in the middle the way we used to when I was little and couldn't sleep.

But it's not a choice, not really. Not with what's at stake.

"No thanks," I call back.

"Okay. Night, then."

I swallow. "Night," I reply weakly, and then wait to see if he'll hear something off in my voice. I'm not sure if I'm disappointed or relieved when his footsteps retreat to the couch.

Deep breath. I toss the tablet in my backpack, sling it over my shoulder, and slip out onto the fire escape.

CHAPTER
FIVE

ISH N' CHIPS IS THE last stop on the bus line and I make it with no time to spare. I probably could've used the subway and saved ten minutes, but being trapped underground is a huge trigger for me and I need all my wits for whatever it is I'm about to walk into. The designated restaurant—"restaurant" probably being overgenerous terminology—is sandwiched between a defunct laundromat and a shady-looking pawn shop. The décor is faded and the air is coated with a fine sheen of grease, fish, and apathy. The rusted bell above the door barely manages a clunky jingle when I walk in.

I stop just inside the doorway to tug my *Last Airbender* beanie down tighter over my hair. Hopefully it'll help hide my identity from any protestors who might wander past. There's a group of them camped out at City Hall just a block to the east, or so I gathered from the chatter on the bus.

I scan the tables in search of the texter. Behind the counter, a dead-eyed waitress watches an ancient box TV tuned to a Spanish sports channel. An exhausted-looking mom scarfs down fries in the corner booth while she watches a video on her phone. When she's not looking, her son feeds chunks of his fillet to the apparently cannibalistic goldfish next to the front register. There are no other customers. Maybe the texter is late? Although I'm not even sure who I'm looking for—it could be the waitress for all I know.

I shift, my hand still on the doorknob. I could bail. I could leave before anyone notices me, forget about the message and hope for the best. I could go home and eat that ice cream. God knows I need it.

"In or out," calls the waitress, still staring at the TV. "You're running up the heating bill."

I pry my fingers off the door and let it creak shut.

Quint slides into a booth and, for lack of a good reason not to, I sit next to him. Crumbs and a fleck of what I hope is ketchup dot the tablecloth, so I keep my hands in my lap. I take a deep breath to steady myself and immediately resolve to spend the rest of my time here breathing as shallowly as possible.

The waitress shuffles out from behind the counter and approaches my table. "What do you want, sweetie? The special is the popcorn shrimp platter." Her words are perky but her tone is as dead as her eyes.

"I don't like seafood," I say without thinking. She raises an eyebrow and I blush. "I'm...meeting someone. Nothing for me right now, thanks." I only brought enough money for the bus fare.

She drifts away with a dissatisfied look. I pick at the tablecloth.

"I think maybe I might've liked seafood," Quint says from my side, but it comes out as a question.

I sneak a sideways glance. He's not looking at me, instead staring out the window into the distance. His eyes are narrow and his jaw is tight like he's locked in some sort of internal struggle. I hesitate, then allow myself just a second to watch him in the window's reflection. If he is somehow real, if he's a ghost or stuck in another dimension or something, what must it be like for him to have no memories of himself? Maybe it's his own brand of ash and rubble.

I look away and pull out my phone, calling up a game to distract myself—and then I stop. A search engine icon is hovering on my home screen, and, before I can change my mind, I press it.

I've never searched for Quint before. I didn't have the

energy to do much of anything in the hospital. But if he really is—or was—real, surely I could find some trace of him. He may not be able to remember his name, but he's a teenager in a lab coat. That should narrow the field at least a little.

I key in "teen scientist" and then add "agency," since he's got to be connected to them somehow, and then I hold my breath and hit search.

The bell on the door jingles. "Red alert," Quint interrupts. "Look innocent."

I jump, hit the exit button before he can see what I'm doing, and look up at the small mob of people bristling with signs, one of which is another blurry picture of me with a red slash through it.

Holy crap. I'm gonna get murdered.

"For the record, not your best innocent look," Quint notes.

I ignore him and do my best to blend into the pleather bench. They've come for me. This was a trap set by Dr. Lila, her threat to dox me carried out, and they've followed my phone's GPS or maybe they sent me the text in the first place and I've made a stupid, stupid choice and I'm going to be kidnapped or beaten or worse. Or maybe someone will call the cops and then Dr. Lila will carry through on her other threat, and Dad is going to be all alone—because God knows Kyle barely bothers to visit—while I rot in prison with nothing but a maybe-real hallucination and no answers. I scan for exits, trying to figure out the best escape route, trying to breathe diaphragmatically and not hyperventilate and cause another damn panic attack—but the group just walks up to the counter and orders shrimp combos and chicken baskets.

The waitress disappears into the kitchen. The group watches TV. She hands them a tray full of food. They take it, go to a corner booth, and start eating.

So...they're not here for me? I glance at Quint; he's cleaning his glasses on his lab coat, deep in thought, frowning like he has no idea what's going on either. I tug my beanie down tighter, shading my eyes with one hand like I'm tired while I think frantically about how to get the hell out of here without them getting a good look at my face.

Someone taps on the window behind me. I twist around before I can think better of it. A napkin is pressed to the glass, scrawled with spidery writing:

Should I tell them who you are?

I freeze.

Behind the napkin, the waning moonlight wraps my texter in a murky silhouette. From the person's shape and the way they hold themselves, I'm guessing it's a guy, but all I can make out is his wrinkled hoodie and the patio table he's sitting at. He timed this for the darkness, waited until the protestors were here to threaten me. Dr. Lila didn't dox me, at least not yet. This is his plan. Blackmail, for the second time tonight.

Fury bubbles up over my fear. I never knew it could feel like this, like there was some kind of fizzy acid in my veins, terrifying and energizing and paralyzing all at once. I don't know what to do with it.

The napkin hovers at the window. The blackmailer waits. Without taking my eyes off him, I get a pen from my bag. I pull a napkin from the dispenser. I hold one to the other, and wait for a way out to present itself.

Ink bleeds into the napkin, spreading in a slow stain.

Quint tilts his head, taking in my paralysis, and then puts his glasses back on. "You could always tell him to go screw himself," he advises with a shrug. "It seems to have worked for you in the past."

Despite myself, I snort, and the fury fades just a touch. The trace of a smile flits across his features, and something else too: triumph. Not only has he succeeded in jolting me out of my frozen state, but he's finally gotten me to acknowledge him, even if it wasn't with words.

My lips flatten out. I look away and hunch over the table—I can still hardly stand to meet his eyes—and then lift the pen. *What do you want?* I scribble, and press my message to the glass.

On the other side of the window, the napkin vanishes. The texter tilts his head in the direction of my backpack.

My pulse skips a little faster. The tablet. He wants the tablet.

Outside, streetlights flicker. A burst of wind rattles against the window and shakes the striped umbrella over the blackmailer's head while I try to figure out my next move.

Maybe if I make him angry I can get him to come closer, show himself. I doodle on the napkin, taking my time before I hold it up again: *Go screw yourself*, decorated with tiny smiley faces.

Now it's Quint's turn to snort.

The blackmailer pulls his napkin away, writes on it, lifts it back up.

5, it says. I blink at him. He takes it down, writes again, presses it to the window.

4.

He flips the napkin over: *3*.

I shove out of the booth and lurch to my feet. A countdown. He's giving me a countdown. Three seconds to give him the tablet, three seconds before he rats me out, three seconds before I get mobbed.

I drop my napkin, heart racing. I won't give him the tablet. I can't. It's the only lead I've got.

But the data is corrupted anyway. And would Mom want

me to risk my life, to risk Dad being alone, just to prove she was a good person? I shouldn't need proof to know that. I am a terrible person to need proof to know that.

Tears stinging the corners of my eyes, I scoop up the tablet and head for the door.

"Wait!" Quint calls, jerking out of his seat, eyes on the tablet—but I'm already gone.

I reach up to cover my face when I walk past the protestors, pretending to scratch my ear. The bell jingle-clunks when I walk out. The low rumble of distant thunder clatters up against the buildings and another breeze snaps past, the smell of salt and rain tangled together. A storm is coming in from off the coast. Pedestrians hurry past, eyes on the sidewalk or on their phones, trying to reach their destinations before the weather goes bad. No one notices me. No one notices the blackmailer.

I turn. The moon is nothing more than a silver smear behind the clouds now, but the blackmailer's table is only a few feet from a street light. If I can get close enough, if I can make him turn around, I can get a better look and maybe I'll still have a shot at figuring out who he is and how he knows about me—

The writer scribbles something on the napkin, gets up, and walks away. Cautiously, I step closer.

Leave it here, it says.

I weigh the tablet in my hands and stand there for a

long moment, trying to think of some magical option that doesn't end with me dead or in jail.

"Please," Quint says.

I almost glance at him but catch myself just in time.

He inhales, hesitates. Exhales. At the edges of my vision, his hands clench and unclench. "There's got to be another way," he says at last. The words are unsteady, fumbling. It's the first time he's ever sounded anything but composed. My resolve weakens the tiniest bit and my gaze flits to him, but he's got his eyes closed like he's concentrating on finding exactly the right words. There's a worry crease between his brows and it makes him seem suddenly, unsettlingly...human.

I tear my gaze away. I'm the one who'll pay the price for whatever I decide to do next. I have to make this choice for myself, and not for a guy who may or may not be a figment of my own imagination.

Quint lifts one hand toward the tablet but stops short of touching it. "That thing is my only shot at figuring out how to get my life back," he says. "Please, just—talk to me. We can get it to work, we can figure this out. I swear we can."

I bite my lip. I consider his plea. Then, because there is no other way, I lay the tablet gently atop the napkin.

And then I retreat thirty feet, duck into a side alley, and pull out my phone. I turn off the flash and the shutter noise and zoom in as far as I can, and when the blackmailer strides out of the shadows and snatches up the tablet, I snap five pictures of him in rapid succession.

The blackmailer slips back into the darkness. I lower the phone. Then I turn and, unable to help myself, look Quint in the eye. I wait for his judgment and try to pretend I don't care what it is.

He meets my gaze. He blinks and then, slowly, smiles: a thoughtful, cautious thing, but somehow more real than anything else he's shown me of himself. "Interesting," is all he says, and his eyes are narrowed ever so slightly in a way that says he's reevaluating me.

The worry line is still there, though—and I'm kind of glad. Somehow it manages to make me feel just a little bit more at ease, proof that I'm not the only one thrown off-kilter by this whole situation.

Plus…it's actually a little cute.

Shouting jars me out of my thoughts. Inside Fish N' Chips, the protestors are standing, crowding around the TV. Unease brushes at me—something about the way they move, jerky and clenched—and I can't help but edge closer to the front window to see what they're watching.

A newscaster speaks in rapid-fire Spanish while the camera shot pans to show the horde of protestors still at City Hall. They're riled up about something, screaming and shaking their signs, crowding the metal barriers. One of them tries to kick a police officer. I inch closer, my worry growing as I catch enough of the newscaster's muffled Spanish to translate a few words that I remember from my ninth-grade languages class: information. Riot. The feminine for traitors.

Two pictures flash in the bottom corners of the screen. One is a photo of me from last Christmas. I'm in my ratty old Gryffindor sweater, arms thrown around two of my ex-friends, snow in our hair and mugs of cocoa in our hands. Their faces are blurred out, but mine is clear as day.

In the other corner is a picture of my mother wearing her agency uniform and standing in front of an American flag.

I stop breathing.

One of the protestors snarls and slams a fist down on the counter. "Terrorist bitches," he growls, and the moment goes suddenly crystalline. All I can hear are his words. All I can see is that picture of my mom. The moment stretches tight and shatters. As if someone else is controlling my body, I take two steps, yank the door open, stride up to the counter, and punch him in the face.

We stare at each other. He puts a hand to his nose. I look down at my fist. It's shaking. It's bloody. His blood, but mine too. There's skin scraped off two of my knuckles from where I caught his teeth. I don't feel it. All I can feel is the rage, but even that is at a distance, like it exists somewhere outside of my head.

I look back up. The man I punched is still holding his nose, gaping at me. I lift my hand and stretch out my fingers. They're slender. Chewed-off nails. One has a ring, which Dad gave me for my sixteenth birthday. I know my hand, this is my hand, but it just did a thing it's never done before and that felt…

Right.

And that feels so, so wrong. I hate violence. I've always thought it was the easy way out. I come from a family of doctors, I want to be one too, and we don't hurt. We heal.

Earlier I was so afraid when I thought maybe I didn't really know my mother, but now—now I don't know me.

I whirl around and flee. Out the door. Down the side-walk. There's a trash can outside the pawn store next door. I grab it just in time to throw up. When I'm done, the pro-testors are at the door of Fish N' Chips, yelling. One of them calls me by name. I'm so shaky I can barely stand, but I still run, breath coming in frantic gasps, fury drowned out by a blistering panic attack, until I find the bus at a stop two blocks west. I squeeze between the closing doors, find a seat all the way in the back, and huddle into myself. The bus rumbles down the street, leaving the protestors in its smoke.

Quint sits next to me. He doesn't say a word.

I lift my hand again. I know this hand, I tell myself firmly. And I know me. So I got angry. I've been through a hell of a lot in the last few weeks, don't I deserve a little anger?

But I've never been angry like this. It's not right, feeling this way. That protestor had probably lost someone in the explosion. Maybe a spouse. Maybe a kid. He didn't know my mother, knew nothing about her beyond her picture on the TV with a newscaster calling her *la traidora*. He'd made a totally natural snap judgment. And I'd punched him for it.

I put my head down against the back of the seat in front of me and breathe deeply. The panic starts to fade, but that scares me even more, because I don't know if that unthinking anger is still beneath it or not. When a sweet older lady across the aisle notices my distress and offers me a bottle of water, I take it. Think. I need to think. Get back on track— prove Mom's innocence, figure out what Quint is and how to get rid of him. When that's done, I'll feel like myself again.

I pull my phone out of my pocket and thumb it on. A sense of purpose settles inside me and I grab onto it with both hands. The pictures I took of the blackmailer are blurred and shadowy, but they're proof. And I know exactly what to do with them.

CHAPTER SIX

B Y THE TIME THE BUS drops me off halfway across town, clouds have crept over the sky and drowned out the last few stars. Street lamps cast pools of orange light across the sidewalk, but darkness is seeping in around the edges, muffling the shadows, hiding the raindrops that have begun to freckle the pavement.

The bus lumbers away. The exhaust fumes dissipate. With one hand clenched tight around the phone in my pocket, I turn toward the sidewalk and steel myself.

A boy sits at the bus stop bench. He's long and lean, legs propped up on the seat of a motorcycle, a single earring glimmering in the twilight. He's got a pencil between his teeth and he's staring at a crossword puzzle on the back of a newspaper he can't possibly be able to see.

"You had an imaginary friend when you were seven," he says, not looking up. "Mr. Wiggles, you called him. I guess it's too much to hope your current hallucinations are just a relapse." He takes the pencil out of his mouth and licks the tip. "What's a five-letter word for 'you're standing in my light'?"

Quint raises an eyebrow, examining the boy on the bench. "I kind of like him," he muses, "and I also kind of want to punch him," which pretty much sums up every-one's relationship with my big brother.

I sigh and slide onto the bench, not quite managing to keep the edge out of my voice. "Good to finally see you too, Kyle."

Category 5, I'd texted him ten minutes ago—our code for "emergency." I need help.

Admitting it is the first step, he'd replied. And then, *meet me at 49th and Maple. Bring snacks.*

Kyle glances up and observes my empty hands. "I see you've reneged on your part of the deal."

But I've had a hell of a night already, and I've been forced to find Kyle when I so desperately wanted him to find me, and the residue of my earlier fear and anger has left me too exhausted to pick my battles like I normally would—so I cut straight through the bullshit. "You weren't at the memorial service," I say flatly.

The words burn on the way out. For me, Mom's death

is a gaping wound. For him—going about his daily life, too wrapped up in his own world to even call—it's a weeks-old tragedy that's apparently already started healing. I hate him for that and, even more, I hate that a part of me is desperately jealous of it.

His lazy grin vanishes. Taking his time, he flicks the pencil around in his fingers, drops it into his pocket, and folds the newspaper. By the time he looks up, the grin is back, though it's a bit sharp around the edges now. "Neither were you. And I was busy with training."

My gaze skates over the gun-shaped lump beneath his jacket. My big brother, hacker and all-purpose troublemaker turned agency recruit, who's been so busy training for his new job he couldn't be bothered to spend more than a few hours at his unconscious sister's bedside.

He sees the direction of my gaze. His eyes narrow. "What exactly was it you needed my help with?"

I look away. Has he heard what the news said about Mom and me yet? How much can I tell him without making him go all overprotective big brother? I pick my words carefully. "I'm kind of in trouble."

"And you need me to get you out of it? Gotta love the role reversal, at least." But he's sitting up a little straighter, scanning me for injuries or signs of duress. I slip my wounded hand in my pocket before he can spot it. "Is it about the panic disorder? Or the hallucinations—are they getting worse?"

I'm not sure how much he knows about Quint. Kyle has been an agent for a few months now, but he's mostly just an analyst. He probably doesn't have high enough security clearance to know more than what I've told Dad, which isn't much. "Not exactly," I answer. I pull out my phone and thumb it on, showing him the pictures of my blackmailer. "I need you to find out who this is. He stole something from me and I need to know why. You've got access to software that can clean these up, right?"

Kyle frowns, flicking through the photos. I should be looking at the phone, but I've got all the pictures memorized already and I haven't seen my brother in months. I can't take my eyes off him—he looks the same, all dark eyes and messy hair and lazy snark. But something about his energy is different, older. His humor feels whittled down now, pointed and purposeful, like he's laughing at himself instead of the world and also like he isn't really laughing at all.

"Is he carrying?" Kyle interrupts my thoughts, tilting the screen at me. The blackmailer is turned halfway and his hoodie pocket gapes open to show a glimmer of bright, blurry metal. Kyle's still looking at the phone, but his jaw is tight and he's got a dangerous glint in his eyes.

"I don't know," I answer. "He didn't threaten me with a gun, anyway." He didn't have to.

The dangerous glint eases a tiny bit. Kyle turns the screen off. "What did he take? You should just report it and collect the insurance. Most stolen goods never get recovered anyway." He's shutting down already, picking his newspaper back up and holding the phone out to me, going distant again now that he's decided my situation isn't dire enough to require his aid.

"I could go to jail," I say softly.

He doesn't move. He closes his eyes and breathes out. "What have you done, Cam?"

"Lifted an agency director's tablet."

His eyes open. The storm rumbles to the west, and a few fat raindrops splatter against the pavement at our feet. He pockets my phone, grabs a helmet from the bike's seat, and tosses it to me.

"Get up," he says, his tone flat. "I'm taking you home."

———

Thunder rips through the sky behind us, rattling my bones up against each other as the bike slides around a corner. "Can't you afford a car now?" I shout, clutching my brother's waist. I don't really expect him to answer, since I've been trying to coax him out of his silence for the last ten blocks with no result, but this time he humors me.

"Cars are for weaklings," he yells over his shoulder with

a smirk that almost looks real.

I tighten my grip around his ribs and my scabbed-over knuckles twinge in response. "Dry, safe weaklings who don't take corners at forty-five degree angles," I mumble. I know the basics of riding a motorcycle—Kyle forced me to learn so I could take my road test, which I failed miserably last fall—but the constant leaning and the lack of any sturdy metal separating me from the cold hard asphalt makes it my least favorite mode of transportation. Also, I think I swallowed a cricket.

He pulls to a stop at the curb and I stumble off the bike, trying to look stoic while also physically restraining myself from kissing the pavement.

Kyle claps me on the shoulder as he passes. "Indoorsy as ever, I see." But that odd edge is still behind his words, like his mind is already miles away.

I unsnap my helmet and frown, looking up at the building in front of us. "I thought you were taking me home." This place is dingy and gray, with bars on the windows and train tracks out back. COASTAL GLORY STATION, boasts the sign above the door. We're not that far from our apartment building—maybe he's got an errand to run here, one of his shadier-than-normal acquaintances to meet? That might give me more time to figure out how to convince him to help me before he drops me at our doorstep and rides off into the night without a backward glance, which I'm pretty sure is his plan.

But he pulls open the glass front door and motions at me to go in with him. "I am," he says. "My home."

I freeze. My brain scrambles for something to say while I buy time to work out what's happening. "You've been living in a train station? No wonder you wanted me to buy the snacks," I say, but the words come out wrong, strung tight like beads on a necklace.

He doesn't say anything, only waits there at the door.

I plant my feet. "Kyle, what's going on?"

He gives me a thin smile. The edge is gone from his words now, replaced by a resigned sort of certainty. "I think it's best if you come stay at the Washington base with me until your situation settles down," he says. Lightning flares overhead, and a gust of wind rattles against the door he's still holding open.

The Washington base. That means he transferred out of state and I didn't even know.

I grit my teeth and force myself to focus. His plan is logical—if overprotective—but I have to figure out how to talk him out of it anyway, because there's no way I'll be able to discover anything about Mom or my condition in Washington. I'd be stuck on the base all day every day, constantly watched by Kyle and surrounded by agents. It would be just as bad as jail—which, lest I forget, is still a possibility once Dr. Lila discovers her missing tablet. "No," I tell him, and try to sound firm.

But Kyle is five years older than me and he's been winning our arguments since before I was born. "Yes," he says simply. The "or else" doesn't need to be spoken—he'd change his mind about me being safer at an agency base if he knew she'd threatened me.

I consider telling him what Dr. Lila said about Mom being a suspect but the words stick in my throat. He's an agent, after all. I have to be sure he'd pick my side before I make him choose between believing me and believing them.

I try a different tactic. "It's a tough time for me. I need to be at home."

"No, you need to stop doing stupid things, and apparently that's not going to happen if someone isn't around to keep an eye on you twenty-four seven."

A trickle of anger slices through my worry. I narrow my eyes. "If you wanted someone to be around maybe you shouldn't have abandoned me when I needed you most, jackass." I want to stuff the words back inside as soon as they leave my mouth but Kyle doesn't even break eye contact.

"That's the mistake I'm fixing now," he says calmly, and waits for my next protest.

I grasp for another argument, any other way out of this. Quint's been loitering in the background, but now he steps to my side and leans in. "Your dad," he says. "He'd never go along with sending you out of state, not right now."

"Dad!" I say, and even I can hear the relief in my too-loud voice. "Dad won't let me go. What exactly are you planning on telling Dad?"

Kyle's fingers tighten around the door handle. "*You* are going to tell him that this is the best thing for you right now. You are going to tell him that you want this. You are going to tell him that you need to see some different doctors, work more closely with the agency, be more active in your recovery."

A sinking feeling slides through my stomach even as I speak. "And why would I do that?"

"Because if you don't," he says, and his eyes go sharp and his smile drops away and suddenly everything about his expression is tight and stark and wrong, "I will tell him the truth, which is that you're sabotaging yourself, that you're committing felonies, that you're messing around with dangerous people, and that I'm not going to let you screw yourself over. You're coming to Washington with me so I can keep an eye on you because, Camryn, I will not lose another family member this month."

A burst of wind scatters raindrops over us. Lightning cracks through the sky overhead, a brilliant blue-on-black spider's web. I stare at Kyle. He stares at me. There's no snark in his tone, no lazy grin on his face.

My brother is serious, and I am well and truly screwed.

He sees my realization and straightens, a tired sort of victory settling over him. He pulls out his wallet. He snags a few dollar bills and hands them to me, then tosses me my phone. "You have five minutes to call Dad," he says. "Meet me at the ticket booth."

I look down at the phone. It's a concession, in its own way. Kyle doesn't trust me enough to let me stay in town, but at least he's not going to call Dad and tell him that himself.

I hold up the money with numb fingers. "What's this for?"

He gives a humorless smile and jerks his head at the vending machines past the entryway. "The snacks," he says. "It's going to be a long ride."

He strides into the station. The door swings shut behind him.

Thunder rumbles long and low, a warning that I should get inside too, but I don't move. I stand rooted to the side-walk, a borrowed helmet under my arm, a phone in one hand and a handful of crumpled dollar bills in the other, and try to think of what I'm supposed to do now.

"He's got an agency ID in his wallet," Quint says from behind me. I jump; I'd almost forgotten he was there. He's leaning against the wall with his arms crossed like he doesn't have a care in the world, but his eyes are fixed on my broth-er's retreating back. "It looked like it works as a key card too," he says, like it's just a casual observation.

I frown at him. The wind picks up, whistling through the buildings, goading me. Slowly, I turn to follow his gaze. Kyle is at the ticket booth now, knocking on the window for the attendant, flipping his wallet open and shut. I spot a glimmer of green and white near the fold.

An agency ID. One of those could get me into non-civilian buildings, into the agency's lower-level computer labs, into their facial recognition database. It could tell me who my blackmailer is. It could help me track him down and get the tablet back, and if I can guess Kyle's password, maybe it could even help me restore the corrupted data.

Kyle turns, and I whirl away before he can see me staring at him. No. Of course I wouldn't steal his ID. How could I even be considering it? That could get me in even more trouble than I'm already facing, and get my brother fired. I just punched someone for the first time half an hour ago and now I'm considering stealing from my own brother? I won't do it. I won't be that person.

But Quint pushes off the wall and shrugs one shoulder. "Maybe getting him fired wouldn't be so bad," he says, reading my mind. "I've seen how much you miss him. I was there all the times you pulled up his contact info but couldn't quite bring yourself to hit the send button. If you do take that card, they might fire him...but then he'd be home. And you could be one step closer to knowing the things you need to know."

Fire laces through my veins, because the picture he's painting—I want it. I want it so badly that I turn back around and watch my brother again for thirty long seconds, weighing the possibility, debating.

And then I lift my eyes. To Quint, who's standing just a little too close now, with just a little too much intensity in his gaze. And for the first time, I consider the implications of him. For the last week I've been treating him like an unsettling-but-harmless daydream, but what if he isn't? What if for the last eight days, while I've been ignoring him, he's been learning me? He's telling me to betray my brother, and he knows exactly what to say. He knows exactly how to make me want it.

I look at Quint and, for the first time, I wonder if I should be worrying less about whether he might be real and more about whether he might be dangerous.

"Cam!" I jump; it's Kyle, cracking the door open to shout at me. "Get a move on, the storm will be here any minute."

I hesitate for a second longer, looking from him to Quint, and then I clear my throat. "Give me your wallet," I say, and somehow the words come out normal. "If I'm going to be on a train with you all night, I'm gonna need a hell of a lot more than three dollars' worth of Twizzlers."

He rolls his eyes, but relief eases his expression. He

thinks I've given in, that I'll go along willingly, that the two of us are okay again. And he's so relieved thinking it that he pulls out his wallet, tosses it over without question, and turns back around without wondering whether the girl who's just stolen an agent's tablet might be willing to steal from him too.

"Hurry up and call Dad," he calls over his shoulder. "Our train will be here soon."

Numb, I wrap my fingers around the wallet. "Okay," I say. "I'll just be one more minute."

CHAPTER
SEVEN

WHEN I HAND THE WALLET back to Kyle, I'm certain he'll discover what I've done. The weight of it will be off, or there'll be dents in the leather where my fingernails dug in, or his big brother radar will tell him there's a guilty catch in my voice that means I've transgressed. So I try to put him on the offensive instead.

"Dad got called in for another half-shift, but he'll bring up your bike and some of my things this weekend and stay with us for a bit," I tell Kyle as I drop the wallet and a bag of Funyuns into his waiting hands. "But he wants to know why you happened to be in town today. Since you've been living out of state without telling him, and all."

The wide open room echoes with my words. The

teeth-rattling storm that's now raging outside has ensured that the station is mostly empty tonight, with the exception of a lone security guard who's shooting a suspicious glance in my direction every few minutes. The surgical implants in my leg and shoulder—courtesy of injuries sustained in the explosion, or so I'm told—set off his metal detector when I came inside, and he's apparently still second-guessing whether I might actually have a pipe bomb hidden in my shoes. The fact that I'm traveling with a guy who's licensed to concealed carry doesn't seem to be helping my case, either.

Kyle winces at my question, leaning against the ticket booth's counter. "I was spending the weekend for a…bowling tournament," he tries, and I raise an eyebrow. "A girl?" That's more likely, but he's still not meeting my eyes. "Cliff diving," he mutters at last, sliding the wallet into his pants.

I let out a slow breath. My plan worked. His ID is in my pocket, and he has no idea it's missing. I should feel relieved and probably guilty now, but did he say cliff diving?

He turns back toward the ticket booth and dings the bell for service, then clears his throat. "The data wasn't corrupted," he says, his voice low.

My brain is still stuck on the cliff diving comment—it drove Mom up the wall that he was into the dangerous sport for a while when he was a teen, and it seems like a bad sign that he's taken it up again now—so it takes me a second to register his words. "What?"

He shifts his weight and tugs at his coat sleeve, like the room is suddenly too warm. "The data. When you tried to look at the files on the tablet it probably said they were corrupted, right?"

Quint stiffens at my side and I resist the urge to look at him. "How do you know that?" I demand instead, leaning closer.

"Encoded high-level agency data is only readable from inside an agency building," Kyle answers, keeping his eyes on the bell. "Try to open it when you're not connected to their network and you get that pop-up. It's possible to unlock the files so you can send them to another computer and read them from anywhere, but it's a bit of a workaround and you'd still need to be connected to an agency network to do the actual unlocking anyway. I just thought you might like to know...whoever blackmailed you won't be able to open the files either, not without access to their intranet. Your medical data or whatever it is you were trying to get, it's safe."

He sends me a hesitant sideways glance, and I recognize his words for what they are. This conversation is his version of an olive branch. He can't say he's sorry so he's giving me this instead—this information that he probably isn't allowed to tell me, in exchange for abandoning us three weeks ago and dragging me to Washington now.

I fold my arms. "Safe," I say, and the word scalds my

throat. He thinks I'm safe from the blackmailer, safe with the agency. And here it is: a test. Is my brother on my side, or has he been fully converted to his employer's? Maybe I didn't have to steal his ID. Maybe there's still a chance he'd help me of his own free will.

I put my hand in my pocket, cupping the keycard. My throat aches, but I swallow hard and keep talking because I have to know. "So you think the agency is trustworthy, then?"

He lifts his head, his expression going flat. "They were good enough for Mom and they're good enough for me. You, though—you're starting to sound just like those protestors."

The words are a slap in the face. I jerk back, stumbling over my reply. "I'm not siding with the protestors. That's not what I meant!"

"Then what did you mean? That you think Mom might've been part of some twisted agency conspiracy, that she lied to us every time she told us about her day?"

His words are toneless, hollow, the way they would be if he'd been practicing the words in his head every day for the last month. The way they would be if he was trying to pretend they weren't something he was afraid, deep down, could be true.

He works for the agency. Of course they would've informed him, questioned him, as soon as a family member became a suspect. They told him Mom might've been a conspirator…and he thinks they might be right.

I stare at him. Surely he couldn't think that. Not really. "Of course not," I fumble. "She—she would never. I was talking about the agency, not her!"

He looks back at his hands, expression still flat. "She was the head of the psychiatric research division. She had one of the highest clearance levels on the base, she knew everyone's psych profiles, she would've been number one on a terrorist's recruitment list. If the agency was untrustworthy or doing something unethical, she would've either known about it and put a stop to it or she would've been involved in it. And she didn't put a stop to anything, did she?"

The room is closing in on me. "No. That's not true. Maybe her superior ordered her to work on a project and she didn't know what it was, or something. Even if the agency is hiding something, that doesn't mean she's guilty! We would've known if she was the kind of person who could do something terrible on purpose."

I clam up. I'm not sure when I stopped trying to convince him, and started trying to convince myself.

He doesn't look at me. The silence crackles and burns between us, an invisible electric current, and I understand. There's nothing else I can say to him. He's too scared, scared that the newscaster is right, scared to find out we're wrong.

He would never help me look at the tablet, because he thinks he knows what we would find.

My brother is more afraid than I am.

I take my hand out of my pocket and lay it on the counter, empty. Quint turns away. I don't look to see what expression he's wearing, because I don't want to know if he thinks I'm right.

Kyle sighs and dings the bell one last time, glancing into the apparently vacant ticket booth. "Did they send everyone home?" he mutters, and motions at the storm outside. "They had to shut down their subway stop for flooding. Hopefully the last aboveground train makes it through, or we might be in for a long night. Or, you know, longer than it's already been." He shoves the bell away and turns, scanning the room for an employee.

Still distracted by our conversation, I glance into the booth. A computer, a chair, a few shelves, a shoe...

I blink. The shoe is lying sideways, half obscured behind a shelf.

And it's twitching.

I flounder, try to form words for a few seconds before I finally smack Kyle in the arm to get his attention. He frowns at me. "If you're resorting to violence now, you should probably keep in mind I'm learning jujitsu and you can't throw a punch without straining something," he says, and I flinch and shove my hand in my pocket again to hide my bloody knuckles, but he doesn't notice.

I use my other hand to point at the shoe, just in case.

He follows my gaze and his façade of humor falls away like a dropped mask. He takes a step back, searching for the security guard. "Hey!" he yells. No answer.

Whoever's attached to that shoe could be having a heart attack, a seizure, a stroke. I grab the doorknob and try to twist. Locked. I knock hard on the window. "Are you okay?" I shout through it, but the shoe doesn't move.

I yank at the knob again, rattling the door in its frame with no results, forgetting to hide my hand from Kyle. "Damn it, open up!" No one answers.

Kyle edges me aside. He pulls out his wallet—I go stiff, but he only grabs his driver's license without noticing the missing keycard—and jimmies the lock. "Misspent youth, don't fail me now," he mutters. The lock clicks open. He slides to his feet and shoulders his way into the room.

I'm right on his heels. Adrenaline pounds through me, focusing my anxiety to a pinpoint purpose. Dad's had me CPR certified for years and my training is kicking in, urging me to get to the body *now*, to check pulse, breathing, pupils.

Kyle reaches the body first and pulls out his phone. "Cam," he shouts, because he never cared to learn first aid, but I'm already on it. I skid around the corner of the bookshelf and drop to my knees. The guy on the floor is old, maybe late sixties, the grandfatherly type with an old-fashioned trainmaster hat and a front pocket full of lollipops. I shake his shoulder and shout: no response, no breathing. I snatch up his wrist. His pulse is thready and arrhythmic. There's no blood, no visible wounds. I lift his sleeve, searching for a medical ID bracelet that could tell me if he has a condition. No luck.

His eyes snap open, search the room. Lock onto mine.

I freeze.

Something is wrong. Something in his eyes is…wrong, missing, empty. Like he's already gone.

Under my fingers, his heartbeat flickers.

"Don't," I whisper, but the word sticks in my throat.

———

Once upon a time, my mother told me that souls leave a mark when they pass out of this world. They dance like falling stars, twisting through the night, and then gather all their energy to launch themselves in a final brilliant flash into heaven.

She was being poetic, but she was wrong. There's no light, no mark, no beauty. It's just someone who's there one moment and not there the next, and it's the most terrifying thing I've ever witnessed.

———

Quint is at my shoulder. "Something is wrong," he says, staring down at me.

The words yank me back into myself and I suck in a breath. How long have I been kneeling here, staring at a dead man?

Okay. Okay. One hand over the other, middle of his chest, right below the sternum. Fingers interlaced. Elbows slightly bent.

When you start CPR, you're making a commitment. Dad's training echoes in my mind. Two compressions per second. I count down from thirty so I'll know when to start rescue breaths. *Until help arrives or the victim wakes up, that's your patient.*

"Breathe," I mutter, but I'm not sure who I'm talking to.

Twenty five. Twenty four.

"Something's off," Quint says again, but I tune him out because I need to concentrate.

"Kyle!" I shout over my shoulder.

"Ambulance on its way!" he shouts back, the barest hint of panic woven through his voice. Neither of us have seen someone die before. Is this how it was for Mom? For all the dead agents? I flinch away from the thought.

Twenty. Nineteen.

My own heartbeat thunders and roars, making my fingertips buzz.

Sixteen.

The edge of something hard is digging into my palm with each compression—a notebook or something beneath the man's vest. I readjust around it, but now the compressions are too high to be effective. I pause for a precious second to sweep the vest aside and yank the object out. I'm about to toss it aside when I register what it is.

A tablet.

Black. Sleek. *Property of Dr. Evette Lila, U.S. Army* engraved on the front.

Clunk. It hits the ground, skids a few inches, and slides to a stop against my knee. I try to inhale, but nothing comes. How did a dead man get my stolen tablet?

The answer sears through my mind:

This is a trap.

I stare down at my patient, agonizing for a long moment, and then I scoop up the tablet and scramble for the door.

Quint stays where he is, crouched above the body with his head bowed. "Camryn," he says, very calmly, "either this man has a light-up belt buckle, or you just activated a bomb."

CHAPTER
EIGHT

THE AIR FLASH FREEZES AGAINST my skin. I stagger to a stop in the doorway and follow Quint's gaze. An array of tiny green lights peek out from beneath the dead man's shirt, stretched in a band across his paunchy stomach and disappearing under his back. Upside down numbers shine dimly through the fabric:

2:00

1:59

1:58

I whirl around, panic screaming in my ears. Kyle is in the doorway, phone plastered to his ear, expression stiff and controlled as he leans out to search for the security guard again. Unable to speak, I lay a hand on his shoulder.

He turns around. Sees the tablet. Looks over my shoulder and sees the lights, sees the timer.

He inhales. Drops the phone. Grabs my hand—too tight, his grip grinding against my fingers. "I'm sorry," he breathes out, because he'd been more worried about saving me from myself than the blackmailer. And then he's pulling me across the station, barreling toward the exit. The doors are right ahead. I get there first, reach out, yank.

Nothing. It doesn't even give an inch. Dead-bolted—we need a key. The security guard is the likeliest person to have one, but he's still nowhere to be found, and this lock looks way too sturdy for Kyle to pick.

"Get back," Kyle orders, and draws his gun. I have barely enough time to spin away and cover my ears. *Crack! Crack!* Gunshot singes the air.

But I don't turn back around to see if it worked, because from this position I can see the security guard—dead, eyes open, slumped against the metal detector.

My God. We're fish in a barrel, and I don't even know who's trying to kill us.

Kyle curses. The gun didn't work. The doors have safety glass.

"The keys, check for keys," Quint urges. I swallow hard, stuff the tablet into my waistband and stride to the body. I avoid eye contact with the dead man as I rummage through his pockets, search his belt. Nothing. His gun is still there, but the key ring is gone.

"Cam, get away!" Kyle spots the guard and hauls me back, but it doesn't matter. We're trapped. My breath comes in rattling wheezes as the panic burns and spirals. If the killer locked the front doors he probably closed off the other exits too, and all the windows are barred. How big will the blast be? The device was small enough to fit on a body, but size matters way less than payload. If the bomb's on a timer, it means the killer had to give himself time to escape, and if he needs time to escape, it means it's gonna be big.

"Tell me you know how to disarm it," I beg Kyle.

"I'm an analyst, not a bomb tech!" He drops my arm and shoves a hand through his hair, turning in a circle, fingers tight around his gun. Then he straightens, grabs my arm again, and pushes me toward the stairs.

The stairs to the subway. Underground, dark, buried beneath yards of dirt. I'll be trapped—just me and the panic.

I yank my wrist from his grip and back away. He stops. He's shouting at me, Quint is shouting at me, but I can't move, I can't breathe, I can't speak.

Kyle reaches for me again. I plant my feet. "What the hell is wrong with you?" he yells, and I cover my face with my hands because that's the question I've asked myself so often and I don't know, except I know something is, and

I'm helpless in the face of it. If I take one step down those stairs, I will die. The fear is too big, too all-consuming, untouchable, unreasonable. Especially now, with everything I've already been through tonight, with no Mom to help me through it.

"I can't," I manage.

Quint steps between us, gets in my face. He ducks his head until our eyes meet. "If your mom's death isn't her fault, then it's your fault. And now," he says quietly, enunciating each word, "you are going to kill your brother just like you killed her."

The world goes silent and electric and all I see are his eyes, full of urgency and apology. Neither is enough. Not for what he's said.

Kyle reaches through Quint, grabs my arm, and yanks hard. Unprepared after the shock of Quint's words, I stumble after him and he drags me down the stairs. SORRY! SUBWAY STOP OUT OF SERVICE, reads the sign on the gate, but the lock gives way under a bullet. Kyle wrenches it open, pulls me through. We scramble over cold turnstiles and into the dark. The whites of his eyes flash when he leans out over the edge of the platform. He pushes me over and jumps in behind me. *Splash.* The murky water is ankle-deep.

I'm choking. There's too much earth around us, burying us, and when that bomb explodes it'll all come crashing down. Kyle shoves his cell phone at me—mine is still in my backpack, sitting uselessly in front of the ticket booth—and I fumble with it until I manage to flick on the flashlight app. Our noise echoes loud and harsh against the walls as we crash down the tunnel. How long do we have left? One minute? Less? Please let us be far enough.

Kyle tugs me sideways. "There!" It's an old maintenance access tunnel, closed off by a heavy metal hatch that looks like something from a submarine. Kyle holsters his gun and grabs the wheel to twist it open. But it's too tight and the wheel is jagged with rust, and when he steps away blood drips down his fingers, shining black in the cell phone light. He wipes his hands on his pants, winces, and then shrugs off his jacket and drapes it over the wheel. He starts cranking at it again, not looking at me. "Listen, if we get separated—"

"Kyle—"

"—keep running. Don't come back for me."

"Shut up and put your back into it," I gasp out. The wheel screeches, turning a fraction. Kyle pulls harder, grimacing. It creaks open. He motions for the cell phone and shines the light in, then leans back.

"Go. It's a ladder, straight down."

He pushes me in. The steel rungs are cold and damp and they scratch my palms as I clamber into the darkness, trying to keep my balance, trying not to think about how much deeper I'm going and how much smaller this tunnel is and how I'm trapped, trapped, trapped. My heart is skipping beats now and I can't catch my breath. I haven't had a panic attack this bad since right before Mom died.

Kyle slings one leg through the doorway and onto the top rung. His earring glimmers when he glances down at me. "Keep moving, I don't think—"

The bomb explodes.

With a sound like the end of the world, a wall of force and fire roars past the hatch. The explosion flings me down, bounces me off the walls like a pinball machine. The hatch slams shut.

Crack. Splash. My head smacks hard against the ladder and then I hit water. I go under. The roar of the explosion cuts to silence. I'm blind and deaf.

And alone.

I claw my way to the surface and drag in a breath. "KYLE!" The scream is serrated, tearing its way out of me.

No answer.

I scrabble at the wall and find the ladder. I can't pull myself up. Something is wrong with my arm, and my back, and my head. The silence is pounding and ringing, and my vision is a wall of shifting shadows. The darkness pulls at me and I can't stop shaking.

Concussion. Shock. Loss of consciousness, shutdown, blackout. I cling to the rung, try to focus, try to pull myself back. If I go under, I'm dead.

But the darkness is relentless, and I hurt everywhere, and it's so quiet.

Quiet. I haven't had quiet in ages, not even in my own head. The isolation of it is sudden and sharp, like lightning. I try to swallow down the name, but the silence is too much and I can't hold it back on my own. "Quint?" The whisper bounces off the narrow walls.

Nothing. The shadows shift, the silence pounds. Then: "I—I'm here." His voice is wrung out and garbled, like someone shouting through a bad connection.

I try to ask him if he can see my brother and how deep is the water and please, talk to me because I think I'm going to die and I don't want to be alone, but the shadows push in against my eyelids and the pressure is too heavy. My fingers slip on the rung.

"Hey! Hold on, you have to hold on!" Quint shouts.

"You can see me?" I slur, squinting. Water creeps into my mouth. I gag and spit it out, but more seeps in behind it. I'm going to go under soon.

Quint's voice echoes against the tight walls. "The cell phone's still on, it's at the bottom of the tunnel. The water's not that deep but you have to stay awake, okay?"

"Children can drown in two inches of water," I recite. Swimming Safety 101. Summer at the beach. Dad holding me up in the water, when I was small and afraid and wanted my floaties.

The ladder is sliding out of my grip. I clutch at it, but it's so slick and my fingers are so clumsy.

A long pause. "Can you not see? You—your head, it's…"

"Kyle," I shout again, but it only comes out as a whisper.

Another silence. "I'm sorry," Quint says, and the sincerity is final, irrevocable. And that's when I remember: you're going to kill your brother just like you killed her.

Oh God, oh God, he was right. And I hate him for it.

I drift.

"Cam, stay awake. Please. Talk to me."

I don't respond.

He tries again. "Look, I don't know what happens to me if you die, but I have no intention of finding out."

"Selfish," I murmur before I can stop myself. The word is fuzzy at the edges, half a dream.

He laughs, a jagged sound of relief. "Yes. And—and a little bit not, maybe."

The shadows flicker and fade into a wall of black.

I try to stay conscious, try to find something to hang on to, but the thoughts float through my mind like mist and I can't grasp any of them. Quint is shouting again,

I think. It fades, weaving in and out like a radio trying to find a signal.

My fingers slip off the rung. Letting go is easy, and the water is cradling me.

I take a breath.

I let it go.

Lights out.

CHAPTER NINE

TWENTY MINUTES LATE, AND I'VE made it as far as the fountain.

The marble is cool beneath my fingers. I've got it in a death grip, trying hard to beat the panic down. The initial attack died out a few minutes back, allowing me to make it through the gate, out of the car, and halfway across the base, but then another one started up and now I'm stranded. Even if I do manage to make it the rest of the way to Mom's office, I might end up with permanent indentations in my palm from this.

Who am I kidding? I'm not going to make it. I should've stayed in bed, stuck to my safe spots, not tried to challenge something that's impossible to beat. If I stay here, the anxiety will never go away. Maybe I wasn't meant to go to college, wasn't meant to get a medical degree. What kind of doctor would I make anyway?

The me from last year believed I'd be a great one just like my parents. The new me has to be more realistic. Maybe I can go to community college, take online classes, find a degree that lets me work from home where I feel safe. It's not my dream, but maybe the new me doesn't have the luxury of dreaming anymore.

I glance at my hand, knuckles white around the fountain's rim. Mom would tell me this is all phobic self-talk, that I need to stop fighting the panic and accept my feelings and act anyway, that the attack won't last forever—but my phone is useless and she's not here to help me and there's no way I can do this without her.

I let go of the fountain and turn back toward the gate.

Boom! The noise is low and ominous like thunder, and the ground ripples. Someone in a lab coat reels into me, sending me farther off balance, and I grab at the fountain to catch myself. With my other hand, I reach out to steady whoever bumped into me. He half-turns and I get a glimpse of light hair and black glasses, and then—

CHAPTER
TEN

WAKE UP DYING.

There isn't any air left, not anywhere in the world, and my body is screaming for it. I manage to choke in half a breath. Air goes in and water comes up.

Drowning. I drowned. Or...almost did?

I roll onto my side on the rough cement and curl into a ball, holding my head, which feels like it's being split open with a rusty axe. My vision is blurry. Someone is kneeling over me. Worried face and blonde hair and green eyes and *you're going to kill your brother.*

I jerk away. I squeeze my eyes shut. If I don't see him, if I don't see where we are, it won't be real.

Rubble. Soot. Ash. Silence. Every time I look at him.

And now this too: a tunnel in the dark. A trainmaster with empty eyes. A wall of force and fire.

"Camryn," he says softly, and the word floats through the darkness like he's making a wish he doesn't want anyone else to hear. That tone, that uncertainty, he said something that same way earlier. What was it?

Selfish, I'd accused. Then he'd replied: And a little bit not, maybe.

Rage boils up. Violence clouds my vision. He has no right to those words, to that feeling. He has no right to pretend to care about me after what he's done. "Get away from me," I hiss. Then, like a dam breaking: "GET AWAY FROM ME!"

My words echo and roil, churning through the narrow tunnel, surrounding me with a wall of sound. My head splits open a little further. I groan and open my eyes.

Quint is kneeling in front of me. One hand is half reached out but he lets it fall, and I don't recognize the stark helplessness on his face until he shuts it down into his normal composed mask.

"That's okay," he says, and his voice is back to smooth-calm-calculated. "Use that. You're going to need it to get us out of here."

I sit up, still clutching my head, something warm and sticky trickling over my fingers. Running on autopilot, my mind tallies up my situation and presents it to me in a neat little list: I have a head injury. A cell phone is flickering in the corner next to a tablet with a cracked screen. My soggy clothing clings and drips, forming a puddle on the otherwise bone dry ground. We're in an elbow shaped tunnel whose only two openings are straight up or out into the darkness.

Phone. The phone. I scramble across the floor and sweep it up, but there's no signal. I'm too far underground. Buried in the dark, beneath a mountain of debris, with a head injury and no one else around except a hallucination I can't bear to look at.

I try the tablet. It powers on but then flickers right back off, damaged from its fall.

I stuff it into my waistband, then stand on shaky legs and turn the phone outward, sweeping its light across the wall. There was a ladder. If I can find the ladder, I can get back to the hatch, and maybe Kyle is up there, maybe the blast wasn't as bad as I thought, maybe there's already a rescue team searching for us. I swallow down the rage and fear, push them away so I can breathe.

But there's no ladder. And no water, even though I was drowning just seconds ago.

"There's something I need to tell you," Quint says from behind me.

I ignore him, because the white noise in my head is getting louder and I think it has a name and I'm scared it might be shock. If that happens to me down here, I'll be nothing but another body for the cadaver dogs to dig up.

Another body. Another. If that tablet meant what I thought it did, if this was all a trap set for me, how many people died for it? Not Kyle. Please, anyone else, the train-master, the guard, civilians, anyone but Kyle. *I will not lose another family member this month*, he told me. I won't either. I can't. Not like this, not again. So until I have proof that he's gone, until someone shows me the…the body—I'll just have to assume he's still alive. It would be just like him, to survive an impossible explosion, to have some snarky one-liner ready for whoever digs him out.

My cheeks are wet. I ignore the frantic tears and continue sweeping the phone's light across the wall in search of the ladder, but I've been over the whole "room" twice now and it's not there. There's only the unreachable hatch twenty feet above.

Quint follows me, trying to make me look at him. "Camryn, stop, listen—"

I whirl on him, drop the phone and swipe my hand through his chest in a savage gesture. I feel nothing, not smoke or mist or a hint of life. That's all he is: nothing. "Shut up," I snarl. "Just shut up. Go away. You shouldn't be here." They're the words I've bottled up for a week, and once I let them out they're a runaway train, impossible to stop.

"Don't you dare give me some damn lecture about Galileo and living in the world and losing people you love. What the hell do you know about any of it? Who even decided you get to be the one to stay when they have to go? How is it fair, that I get you instead of them? And didn't I tell you to get the hell away from me?"

His face is stone. He looks down at his chest, at the spot where my hand swept through him. "This is not how I imagined our first conversation would go," he says, too calm.

"What did you think would happen?" My voice is honed, spiteful. I want him to hurt the way I've been hurt. I know it's not really his fault, I know he might not even be real, but at the moment he's all I've got.

He lifts one shoulder. "That I would say something," he says, "and you would hear me."

The words are quiet and small and they echo around us—not a wall this time, but a plea. I'm all he's got, too.

The fury blinks out. The emptiness from before, from when I was living half-asleep at the hospital, returns. I sag with it. I squeeze my eyes shut. I open them. I brush a hand across my cheeks and finally acknowledge the tears there, and then I flop back against the side of the tunnel, unable to stand on my own. The oxygen burns when I force it into my lungs. "You always know what to say."

He goes tense, sensing the dangerous shift in my tone. "What?"

I drag in another breath. "Everything you say…it's always got a purpose. An intention." My mouth twists. "You're the one who suggested I steal the tablet. Then you talked me into taking my brother's ID, and you knew exactly how to convince me. And just now, what you said about wanting me to hear you—it sounded sincere and maybe it was, but it was as calculated as everything you ever do. You want to disarm me, want me to trust you, want me to do whatever you need me to do so you can figure out what you are, and you don't care that I'm the one taking all the risks in the meantime. I think," I tell him, the realization dawning as I speak, "I think, Quint, that you might be a manipulative bastard."

He puts his hands in his pockets. Takes them out. Then he sighs a long sigh, and his shoulders droop. "Yeah," he admits. "I'm starting to think that myself. If it helps, I don't like it any better than you do. I don't know who I am, but I'm not sure I'd like myself if I did."

I exhale and bend down and scoop the phone up, my bones aching like I'm a hundred years old. "You know the worst part? I can't help but swallow it all anyway. I know what you're doing and it doesn't even matter, because if you are a manipulative bastard, you're a very, very good one."

He tries a smile. "Does that mean you like me?"

I look at the unreachable hatch. I look out into the darkness of the adjoining tunnel. I look back at the boy I'm stuck with, the closest thing I have to a potential ally—if I could trust him. "Tell me something," I say in answer.

"Like what?"

"Something true. Something I could hurt you with, if I wanted."

His gaze drops to the glowing phone in my hand, the only light in the pitch black of our tunnel, and his smile turns bitter and ironic. "I'm afraid of the dark," he tells me. And I hear it: the truth. It's raw and fragile, and he's giving it to me like a gift. Like a peace offering.

"Afraid," I repeat. So we do have something in common.

"I'm afraid of quite a lot of things, actually. Being dead. Being imaginary." He lifts one shoulder. "Being trapped in your head forever."

The tears have slowed now and the anxiety from before, from up above in the train station, is gone. I don't know if it's because this situation is now so far beyond panic or if it just naturally dissipated the way Mom said it always will no matter what I do or don't do.

"I had a dream," I tell Quint, and my words sound a bit steadier now. "I think you were in it."

His vulnerability drops away and he leans in. "What?"

I tell him about the half-memory, the reclaimed snippet

of lost time from the day of the accident. I couldn't quite tell whether the person I'd knocked over was really him, but the glasses and hair made it likely. Which means…what? That he had been alive and was now some kind of disembodied spirit? Or merely that, after a traumatic experience, I started hallucinating about the last person I'd met during it?

He frowns, absorbing. Then he glances up at the nonexistent ladder. "There's something you need to know too. I was gone," he says.

I pull the front of my shirt off my stomach and wring it out. I'm already shivering and the temperature in the tunnel is hovering somewhere around subarctic, and if I don't get dry and warm soon it won't help my odds of survival. "What?"

"You were sinking, drowning. I was yelling but you couldn't hear. You landed right on top of the phone, and then—I was gone. I reappeared, woke up, whatever, just a few seconds before you did. That's why I don't know what happened to the water and the ladder."

I drop my shirt and stare at him. Quint's never disappeared, never slept, never gone farther than a few yards from me. I have no idea what happened or what it means, and suddenly I'm so exhausted, so cold and tired and empty and alone, and I can't bear to spend another minute standing here wondering what the hell is going on.

"Okay," I reply. Then I turn toward the tunnel that

extends into the darkness, hold the phone out in front of me, and take a step. My legs are wobbly and weak but they hold my weight. For now, at least.

"What are you doing?" Quint calls, following as he must.

I grit my teeth at the pain that shoots through my skull with every footstep. "I'm getting us out of this godforsaken hole in the ground," I reply. "I'm going to find my brother. I'm going to get the tablet working and prove Dr. Lila wrong. And then I am going to suppress the hell out of this whole damn day."

He snorts. "Suppression? And here I thought your mom specialized in acceptance techniques."

I stop, turn around. "How do you know that?"

He's blinking, a look on his face like he's seen a ghost. "I...I don't."

I take a painful step closer. "Are you remembering things? Did you know her? Were you a psychiatric intern or something?" If he remembers that day, maybe he can remember what happened—what Mom was doing, what he is, how to get him back into his body or to Heaven or wherever and out of my life.

He shakes himself and strides past me farther into the tunnel. "I don't know," he says, but the words are clipped.

I raise my eyebrows. If I know anything, I know what scared people look like, and right now, he's petrified.

By what? His returning memories? Or by the fact that he's accidentally revealed he does remember something?

He gets to the end of his ten-foot range and stops. I open my mouth—but the phone in my hand chirps, interrupting me. I glance down. *Low power*, it proclaims. *One percent remaining*. There's still no signal and the flashlight app is sucking the life out of the battery. At this rate, we'll run out of juice long before we get close enough to the surface to get a call out.

"Turn it off," Quint says. The words are cold and brittle, a thin sheet of ice to cover whatever it is he doesn't want me to hear in his voice. But it's too late; he's already told me what he's afraid of.

I hesitate. "But you said—"

"Turn it off. You said you wanted to hurt me, right?"

I look down, lift the phone. Press the power button. It leaves a red smear on my brother's screen. "No," I correct, and my voice is softer than I thought it would be. "I said I wanted to be able to hurt you."

"What's the difference?"

The phone warbles sadly to itself, flashes the company logo, and dies.

"Intention," I whisper to the dark.

———

Sometimes, silence has a weight to it—a shape, a feeling, like it's a thing you could hold in your hand instead of just a lack of sound. This type of quiet, it's deep and stagnant. It slides down your throat and seeps into your bones and makes you forget you've ever heard anything but your own footsteps for your entire life.

Quint hasn't said anything in ten minutes.

He's still there. Or maybe he's not. And why should I care? I should hope he's gone, should be glad to finally have my head to myself for a while. I should not be holding my breath, straining to hear him in the dark.

I shuffle onward. Left foot forward. Brace against the wall, shift my weight. Breathe. Right foot forward.

Listen. Silence.

It's like being underwater, this quiet. Deep, stagnant, suffocating.

I clear my throat. "Talking might help, you know. With being afraid. It…helps me, sometimes."

No answer.

"I don't care if you're gone," I call, just to hear myself say it—but immediately wish I hadn't, because even I can hear the lie. And is it really that easy to make me a hypocrite?

"I knew you liked me," says Quint's voice from somewhere to my left. The words are light, but his tone is grim and a little bit muffled, like maybe he's gritting his teeth.

Relief washes over me and is immediately chased by resentment that I should feel relieved. Ugh, emotions. "Try distracting yourself," I offer. "Fighting the anxiety that way is usually counterproductive in the long run, but it might help you get through for now."

"Counterproductive?"

"Yeah." Brace against the wall. Left foot forward. "For panic disorder, which is what I have, fighting the anxiety or trying too hard not to think about it just makes it worse. It means you're treating the anxiety as dangerous instead of just uncomfortable, which freaks you out more, which makes the panic worse, and on goes the cycle of suck. But for you, distraction is probably fine."

"Okay," he says, then pauses like he wants to say something else. I bite my lip—I've hardly told anyone about my diagnosis, and even though he's already heard me mention it at the hospital, it feels different to tell him about it myself. I guess it's only fair, though. He gave me something I could use to hurt him and now I've returned the favor.

"You still there?" I ask after a second.

"I'm working on your distraction technique, trying to think about something else," he answers. "And do you know what I keep thinking? Why a bomb?"

I blink, thrown off course. "What?"

"The blackmailer could've killed you the same way he

killed the security guard. But instead, he set a bomb power-ful enough to level an entire train station. It's like he doesn't only want you dead. He wants you obliterated. Also, why would he follow you to the train station instead of just killing you at Fish N' Chips? I bet there's something important on that tablet. He wanted to see whatever was on that before he decided whether to kill you. So either he didn't know the data would be locked, or he did know and he wanted it anyway—which means he has access to an agency network and has probably already opened the files."

I swallow. "That is a really, really terrible effort at dis-traction. I now feel ten times worse than I did before."

"You told me to distract myself, not you."

"It was in the subtext."

"Is it my fault you're bad at subtext?"

"Shut up," I order, but the banter makes me feel a bit lighter.

He's quiet for a moment. Then, pensively: "I'm not sorry."

The tunnel under my hand falls away; we've come to a T. I stand at the intersection and try to discern which black-ness looks the least impenetrable. My head is pounding and even though it doesn't hurt quite as bad now, it's still hard to walk. I want nothing more than to rest for a moment, but if I sit down I may not get up again. "For your horrendous effort at distraction?" I reply.

"No. For what I said to you on the stairs."

I go stiff. After a second I force my legs to unlock and step into the right tunnel, which doesn't look any brighter, but I think maybe smells a little fresher.

He sighs. The sound of it twists through the dark, wrapping around me. "I know you hate me for it, but all I can think is that I should've said it sooner, should've realized quicker that was the only thing that would get you moving. Then it might've saved your brother and not just you."

My breath hitches and my fingers tighten around the useless cell phone. I think very carefully about what I want to say, and what I cannot bear to say. "You know what it is I hate?" I answer at last. "That look in the trainmaster's eyes. That emptiness. I know that emptiness, or at least a form of it, and I despise it. I hate that it happens to everyone in the end and that every damn one of us is helpless against it. That's the thing I hate."

It's not forgiveness. I can't give him that yet, not when the guilt and truth and uncertainty of what he said is twisted so deep it stabs me every time I move. But it's an understanding, or at least maybe the start of one.

"Is that why you want to be a doctor?" he asks. "So you won't be helpless?"

I stop. "Yeah," I reply slowly. "I think maybe it is, now."

Quint inhales to speak, and then—I realize my hand is

resting not on concrete, but on metal.

I hurry forward, half falling, feeling along the outline of the thing. Metal bars, horizontal in a vertical frame. Rungs. "Quint," I hiss. "I found a ladder."

I lift my foot, test the bottom rung. It holds and so do I, for the moment at least. Surface, here I come. My breathing rattles in my ears as I start pulling myself upward.

"Be careful," he says. I don't reply, because climbing is a hundred times harder than walking—my muscles are already alternating between locking up and trembling uncontrollably. At rung number four, my wrist gives out. I dangle, my whole frame shaking with the effort of not falling, and drag myself back up.

Five rungs. Six. Seven. I hit the ceiling and feel for an exit, praying. My fingers find one crack and then another. It's a square, inset into the roof of the tunnel. Another hatch. And when I hold my breath I can hear the rumble of traffic.

I made it.

I grab the wheel with shaking hands and twist hard, balancing on the ladder. It groans and shudders, but obeys. I heave the hatch up and moonlight pours through like liquid honey. I breathe it in, then look down at Quint. He's grinning at me, his real smile, with his head tilted back and his eyes crinkled at the corners.

I can't help but smile in return. We did it. We made it to

the surface. And from the buildings I can see, I'm less than half a block from home.

My smile fades. Half a block from home. Half a block from finding out who's alive, and who's not.

I shoulder the hatch the rest of the way open and haul myself to the sidewalk. The street is covered in low-lying fog, making the block seem small and isolated even though plenty of cars are still creeping their way through the nearby intersection. A few college-aged guys in a huddled group across the street spot me and one asks if I'm okay, but I turn my back and walk away without a word. I don't want help, don't want police, definitely don't want to be sent to the hospital again. I want to go home. I want my dad, and my room, and my pillow.

And my brother.

I trudge across the street, to where our apartment building rises like a beacon. The lobby attendant blinks and stammers, but I drag myself past her and into the elevator without comment. A middle-aged man starts to step in at my side, gets a better look at me, and then steps right back out.

I mash the fourth-floor button. I lean against the wall, trying to hold myself together. And then I'm standing in front of our door, dripping water the color of old rust onto our welcome mat, inserting my key into the lock and praying.

He'll be here. He will.

Quint looks at me and says nothing.

The door creaks open. I step inside—but the lights are out and the smell is all wrong, musty and stale like a long vacant house. I frown and flick the light switch. Nothing happens. "Dad?" I call, because I can't say my brother's name. I take a shaky step through the doorway, squinting into the darkness.

Slowly, starlight slides across the floor and shows me what's left of my apartment.

The carpet is rolled up and shoved against one wall. The door to my room is missing, hinges hanging askew. Mom's Doctor Who poster is gone. Dad's sci-fi novels are gone. The walls are an unfamiliar shade of beige, and peeling blue painter's tape edges around the windows and door frames. There's no furniture, no dishes in the sink, no heaps of laundry on the ground, only old floorboards that stretch from one vacant room to the next. PLEASE EXCUSE THE MESS WHILE WE RENOVATE FOR NEW TENANTS, says a sign on the wall.

The door swings shut behind me, sealing me in my tomb of a home.

CHAPTER ELEVEN

STAND IN THE NARROW hallway, hands clenched, heart thump-thump-thumping. Breathe. I just have to breathe. This is fine, everything is fine, there's some kind of easy explanation. But Dad is gone and my stuff is gone and nothing is as it should be and I have watched *way* too many reruns of *The Twilight Zone* to pretend this is in any way okay.

I turn to Quint. He's looking at me even though he should be staring at the empty sink, at the blank walls, at the gaping rooms. He needs to say something. He always knows what to say. He'll know how to calm me down, to get me moving, to explain this away.

He doesn't say anything though, only watches me, as

sober as I've ever seen him. Then he steps closer. He leans in, so careful not to brush against me, like he's going to whisper something in my ear.

I blink, standing stock-still, doing my best to not think about leaning into him just a little bit too, closing my eyes and burying my head in his shoulder and maybe, maybe, finally feeling safe.

He's not real and you can't trust him anyway, I remind myself savagely, and don't move a muscle.

Ash-blond hair falls over his glasses as he turns his head to look at a spot just behind my ear. He exhales. "Yeah. It's gone," he says, and steps away.

I blink again, trying to reorient myself now that he's at a safe distance. "What is?"

"The head injury. The three-inch-long gaping wound in the back of your skull, which definitely should not now be a tiny pink scar but somehow is."

"*What?*" I spin away and raise a hand to my head. My hair is too matted with blood for me to feel the injury itself, but there's no pain and now my headache is completely gone.

Mirror. I need a mirror. Four steps and I'm in the bathroom. A paint-splattered drop cloth hangs over the vanity and I pull it down, swiping it across the glass, smearing a wide trough through the dust that coats it. My reflection is washed out, pale and shivering with too-big eyes. I twist and turn. Still can't see the injury.

Two steps. I'm at the bathtub. The faucet is broken and the water is freezing and I dunk my whole head underneath until my scalp stings with the cold. There's no soap. The water turns rusty with old blood.

I tug my hair aside and feel along the edges of the wound. Nothing. Only a thin raised line, like a year-old scar.

I stand up. I pace back into the hallway because the bathroom is folding in around me and I can't sit still. To the door, plastered with its renovation sign. To the sink, empty and gutted. Back again. I close my eyes and cover them with my hands.

Quint clears his throat. "Okay," he says. "Okay. We can figure this out. Just calm down."

I open my eyes, stop in front of him, and stick a finger in his face. "Do *not*," I snap, "tell me to calm down. I am *sick* and *tired* of people telling me to just calm down, like it's something I've never thought of before. This is a situation that freaking *merits* a panic attack, and I will damn well have one if I damn well like."

He looks at my finger, then at me. And then, though he tries to smother it, he smiles.

"Do not smile," I order.

He smothers it slightly more efficiently. "Sorry," he says. "It's just good to see you…" he lifts a shoulder, "alive."

I drop my hand. He's got a look on his face like he's

remembering me in the hospital, remembering me lying in that bed and ignoring him, remembering me running scared in the train station and freezing up on the stairs—and I guess I can understand the smile. I like me better alive too.

I go back to pacing, pulling a hand through my dripping hair. "Alright," I say. "Yes. We can figure this out."

"That's what I said."

I stop in front of him and stick another finger in his face. "Shut up," I order, then rethink. "No. Actually, you're supposed to be some sort of genius," I wave my hand at his lab coat, "so go on. Genius us out of this."

He arches an eyebrow. "Not sure it works like that."

"Then make it work!" I shout. I'm furious at him, at whoever set that bomb, at whatever is causing this impossible situation—but even after my speech about panic being merited, there's only the anger and confusion and a prickling sort of fear, not the otherworldly terror of one of my attacks. I take a breath and try to think straight. "Someone tried to incinerate me. An injury that should've given me a concussion has been somehow healed. My apartment has been miraculously renovated in the space of a few *hours*, and the only family I have left is—" the word chokes off. "—missing," I finish, and press my hands to my eyes again.

He exhales. "Also," he says, "there are no sirens."

I look up. He's standing at the window behind me. "What?"

"No sirens. A bomb went off in the middle of the city twenty minutes ago, and there are no sirens."

I lean out to look around his shoulder. The night is clear, and beyond the haze of the foggy city lights, the stars shine hard and bright like diamonds. Even though we're facing north toward the train station, there's no tell-tale plume of smoke, no wailing ambulances, no fire trucks. And—I didn't notice it earlier because I was so focused on getting home, but the streets are dry. How are the streets dry? It was storming less than half an hour ago, so much that it flooded the whole subway.

But then…the water disappeared. And apparently not just from our maintenance tunnel.

My breath is coming faster and I switch over to my diaphragmatic breathing. Don't break down, not now. Stay angry—but not *too* angry. Think. Think.

My hand goes to the tablet that's still tucked in my waistband. "The tablet," I mutter. "It all comes back to the tablet." Whatever's happening, it all has something to do with the information on that. But I'd need access to an agency network to unlock the files, plus I have no idea if whatever's wrong with it is even fixable.

Kyle would know how to get it working, but Kyle isn't here. He may never be here again.

"Magnetics," Quint muses from behind me.

I twist around to look at him, grateful for the distraction. "What?"

"Magnetics," he says again, his gaze faraway like he's talking to himself. "The tablet. That was the key that set off the bomb—he wired it with a magnetic trigger. As soon as you took the computer a certain distance from the body, the countdown started. He probably keyed the trigger to the presence of your metallic surgical implants too. It's elegant, thorough. It's how I would've done it."

"If you were a mass-murdering psychopath." My voice is too loud, but the blank walls swallow it up.

His gaze refocuses and he winces. "Yeah. That. Sorry."

"Just…" I raise my hands, let them flop back to my sides helplessly—then I remember some of Mom's advice for when I'm feeling overwhelmed. "Let's just focus on the next five minutes. Okay? What should we do in the next five minutes? What's our next step?"

Our. *Our* next step. When did Quint and I get an *our*?

He takes his glasses off and cleans them on his lab coat, which I'm starting to realize is his habit for when he's trying to think clearly. "Well," he says slowly, "the tablet is probably the best place to start."

I'm still flustered from the *our* so my reply comes out sharper than intended. "Great, thanks, Sherlock. I already figured that out, except it's apparently smashed beyond repair."

He cuts me off. "Yeah, but the hard drive might still be intact. If we plug it into another computer, use it as an external drive, we should be able to open the files."

"But we still can't unlock them without access to an agency intranet, which is, inconveniently enough, only located inside agency buildings."

Carefully, he puts his glasses back on. "Yes. That's right."

I narrow my eyes. "You want me to break into one," I accuse. "Break into a government facility, and—what? Hope someone might've left their computer turned on and logged in for us to plug the tablet into?"

"There are some inherent risks to the plan," he admits. "But whatever information is in those files is apparently worth murdering you for, worth exploding a city block for. The longer we go without knowing what that information is, the more likely you are to get killed over it." He shrugs his coat tighter and gives me a humorless smile. "And like I said, I'm not that anxious to find out what happens to me when you die."

I grit my teeth. He's manipulating me again, talking me into committing a felony again. And again it doesn't matter—because he's right. I have no choice. What I do have is a missing family, a hallucination I probably shouldn't trust but somehow keep trusting anyway, and a plan that has about a ninety percent chance of getting me killed, tossed in jail, or tossed in jail and *then* killed.

I cross my arms, uncross them. Rub my temples. Try to think of another way—but there's nothing.

Quint waits silently. He's standing in the hallway across from me now, right under the spot where my family picture used to hang. Its afterimage has been painted over. It makes me want to scrape at the wall, chip away all the ugly new paint and unearth the remainder of my old life. And a foot to his left—that's the spot where our side table stood. I remember Mom's bracelet glinting from beneath the pharmacy bag, tinkling when it fell to the floor. I feel for it in my pocket. Somehow, it's survived the trip through the tunnels: cool, smooth, certain and uncertain, and asking a question I still need to have answered.

My hands curl into fists. I turn my back to the wall, to the echoing living room, to the gaping doorways. I face Quint and take a deep breath.

"Okay," I say. "Lead the way."

———

For an evil lair, the agency's temporary office building on the east side of the city is surprisingly tranquil. The only person visible through the front doors is a lone janitor who seems to be performing some questionable dance moves with a mop to whatever song is playing through his insulated headphones. He's not the only person we have to worry about, though. At least ten windows in the tall glass-and-steel office complex are still glowing, and any one of them could be housing our blackmailer—if he really could open the files, there's a chance he could have agency connections himself.

I wipe my hands on my pants. I've been loitering across the street for the last ten minutes, building up my courage, giving myself a last-second chance to think of a better idea. This is a government building now, which means the punishment for breaking in is likely even steeper than usual. And even though most of the streets in this district are relatively quiet at two in the morning, there's always the chance a patrolling cop or a night shift worker or hell, a particularly scrupulous passing homeless person could catch me sneaking in and bust this whole operation. But a few blocks back I passed an old pay phone and used most of my pocket change to call Dad's cell and Kyle's work phone—because I wanted to believe my brother might answer—and got nothing but one error message and one line that kept ringing until I couldn't stand to listen to it anymore. There's nowhere else I can go. No one else I can trust.

This plan is all I've got.

I wait for the janitor to turn his back and then weave through the thin traffic toward the front doors. A taxi slips around me, stopping one building down to pick up a herd of late-working businessmen. They stride past and I duck my head to keep a low profile, which would work better if my soggy blue and white Chuck Taylors didn't squelch with every step.

"So what's the plan?" Quint asks from my side.

"I thought this was *your* plan," I hiss, stopping to skulk near a bush when the janitor turns back in my direction. Behind me, the businessmen finish squeezing into the taxi and it speeds away.

"No, *this* is walking," Quint replies. "After the walking there will presumably have to be some sort of breaking/entering activity. Which could go very badly if we don't first come up with a plan on how to get inside without the alarms going off."

First an our, now a we. My lips tighten. "I figure that part of the plan mostly involves hallucinatory reconnaissance."

"While you do what?"

"My best imitation of a shrub." I sprint toward a column next to the front door and Quint paces along behind me with an infuriatingly patient expression.

"I was hoping for something slightly more helpful, like 'locate the hide-a-key' or 'look up crime tutorials on YouTube.'"

I give him a look. He pauses, glancing from me to the front door. "Okay," he says suddenly. "I'll go in and check out the security system. But in exchange, please stop calling me a hallucination." He turns and sweeps through the door before I can read the look on his face, leaving me pressed against the column, frowning.

That was—another manipulation? A genuine request? Some strange new combination of both?

Progress, I decide. I think maybe that was progress.

"The janitor's facing the other way," he says, popping halfway back through the entrance. "But they've got all the exterior doors on automatic personnel-only locks."

I give him a grim smile and pull out Kyle's keycard. "I guess I should be glad you convinced me to steal it now," I say, and my voice is more than a little bitter.

He meets my gaze. "I'm not sorry for that either," he says quietly, but the words are laced with apology anyway.

I flash the card at the machine next to the door. It hums to itself. A light glows green and the door unlocks with a *snick*.

The card's plastic edges dig into my palm—I'm holding it too tightly. I loosen my grip, careful not to look at my brother's picture, and slide it back into my pocket next to his phone.

I pull the door open and cool air blasts over me. The burly janitor is bobbing his head a few yards away, baseball cap wobbling in protest atop his bulky headphones. I take a single cautious step. My shoe squishes loudly and I freeze, wincing.

The janitor slaps his mop against the ground and whistles tunelessly.

I hold my breath and lean out, peering at the placards on the opposite wall. Most of the slots are taped over with scraps of paper proclaiming each office's new—and likely temporary—occupant. I search for the name I need, the name that would mean there's a computer here we might know the password to, and find it three slots down and four to the left. Dr. Evette Lila, second floor, office 209.

I exhale, check on the janitor—still scrubbing at a stubborn stain with his back turned—and edge along the wall, shoes squeaking with every move. Five more feet to the adjoining hallway. Four. Three.

The janitor drops his mop into the wheeled bucket, grabs the handle, and starts to turn. I scurry the last few steps and throw myself around the corner. The bucket rattles past without incident.

"…Huh," comes a puzzled grunt a few seconds later. I risk a glance. The janitor is next to the entrance, staring down at a row of muddy footprints. He shrugs, drops his mop back to the ground, and starts up the trail I left behind.

Stupid, stupid. I jerk back into the side hall and grab at the nearest doorknob, but it's locked. Most of them probably are at this hour. The tuneless whistling is only a few yards away now. I lean over, yank off my shoes and socks, and sprint down the hall at full speed. My bare feet pound on the tile. Bathroom, bathroom, there has to be a bathroom somewhere down here.

The hallway dead ends. No bathroom, only a heavy duty door with a vent inset at the bottom. A supply closet.

The bucket rattles into view behind me. With a whispered curse, I twist at the closet's doorknob—praying—and it opens. I throw myself inside and pull the door shut.

Shapes in the dark. Bottles, brooms, bright orange warning cones. The acrid scent of bleach slithers down my throat and burns my eyes. I worm my way through a rack of uniforms at the back, plaster myself against the cold concrete wall, and try to muffle my breathing.

The whistling is right outside the door. The knob turns. A rectangle of light yawns across the room, stopping a few inches in front of my toes. The janitor steps inside, snatches a roll of paper towels off the floor, and turns in my direction.

I look down. The uniforms I'm hiding behind drape to midcalf, but my bare feet are completely exposed. All he has to do is turn a few more degrees to his right and he'll spot them.

Inset into the wall behind me is a sturdy metal shelf. I reach up, grab it, and pull my feet off the floor. My muscles shudder under the strain, but for now, I'm hidden. At least until my grip gives out. Which will likely be soon, judging by my nonexistent levels of physical fitness.

One hand slips. I claw at the shelf, making the uniforms quiver as I regain my grip. Luckily, the janitor is squinting at the writing on the back of a bottle of cleaning solution and doesn't spot the rustling clothing.

Quint folds his arms, staring up at me. "This is a wild guess, but I'm pretty sure you never took any gym classes, right?"

I shoot him a death glare. *Shut up,* I mouth.

"Why? He can't hear *me*."

I amp up the death glare by a few watts. One corner of his mouth twitches in a suspiciously smirk-like expression. I want to throttle him, but at the same time, his snark is at least keeping me from panicking, which was probably his intention, now that I think about it.

The janitor starts whistling again. He rips off a paper towel and dabs at a wet spot on his knee, then strolls back out into the hallway. The door closes with a *click*, but his whistling only retreats a few yards. The mop slurps and splashes as he resumes his cleaning.

So. We're safe for now, but judging by the janitor's prior mopping speed we'll be stuck here for at least ten more minutes while he finishes the hallway.

I release the shelf and lower myself to the floor, rubbing at my aching arms. My eyes sting and burn from the bleach fumes or maybe from sheer exhaustion. I pat my cheeks, trying to force myself to stay awake. My face is cool to the touch and my wet hair is still pasted to my neck, making me shiver.

Quint glances over and then frowns, scanning me more carefully. He clears his throat. "So," he says after a long minute. "Gym. Was I right?"

The last few hours have apparently given him an immunity to death glares, so I jerk my head at the hallway and mime the universal *shush* sign, then add the finger-across-throat *or else* one for good measure.

He shrugs. "He won't be able to hear you through his music, and if you pass out in here you might as well glue a giant 'come murder me' sign on your forehead. Talking will keep you alert till he's gone."

I press my lips together, weighing the options. "The pre-med program at State doesn't require physical education credits and I'm more into books than sports anyway," I whisper grudgingly, then hesitate. The picture that had been on the news earlier, the one of me and my ex-friends from last Christmas—it had been taken at a school trip to a Harry Potter theme park the week before I'd been diagnosed. A few months after that I'd started pushing all my old friends away, too embarrassed and scared to risk telling them what was really wrong with me. And a few months after *that*... I give Quint a sideways glance, then confess before I can think better of it. "I quit school this year anyway. I kept having panic attacks in class so I made my parents switch me to the online program instead."

Shame colors my cheeks. I lift my chin and wait to see what he'll say.

But he only settles down next to me, wrapping his arms around his knees. "Ah."

"Ah? That's it?"

"Were you expecting a lecture?"

"I would lecture me," I mutter.

He folds his hands and doesn't say anything for a moment. "Would you tell yourself that you're ashamed of you?" he asks at last. "That you should be braver, should try harder, should be stronger?"

I pass a hand over my eyes and sigh. By now, those words should be diluted. They shouldn't hurt anymore. They're the same things I've told myself every day for a year, because yes, damn it, I *should* be better. Mom is— was—strong. She got two Ph.D.s and raised a family and even found time to volunteer at the veteran's hospital every weekend. I've wanted to be like her ever since I was old enough to understand how badass she was. And then, what? I turn out to not even be able to sit through my high school biology class because I had a panic attack once on dissection day, and then every time I entered the room I was terrified I'd freak out again. If Mom was the one with panic disorder, she would've kicked its butt on day one.

"Yeah," I tell Quint, and the word comes out muffled because my hand is still over my face.

"Well. You're more ridiculous than I'd realized," he responds.

"Don't hold anything back," I say sarcastically, but I keep my hand over my eyes because they're starting to sting even though I do not, do *not* care what he thinks about me.

"Camryn," he says, and his tone is serious and a little bit annoyed but also oddly gentle, "in the last week I've watched you grieve the loss of people you love, face down two separate blackmail attempts, escape an exploding train station, and break into a government building. And before that, you faced a type of anxiety every single day that most people don't even understand. You are the bravest person I know."

The words sink in, ease deep into a place inside me that I didn't know needed them. I laugh, though it's a little choked. "You're just saying that because you only know two people, and one of them is yourself."

"Yeah," he says, subdued. "That's right."

I drop my hand and look at him. He's staring at the shelves opposite us, and that worry crease between his eyebrows has returned. He shifts, leans his head against the wall, sighs. "I used to hate you, you know."

My spine stiffens. So we're back to this, then.

"I said used to," he adds before I can reply. He lets his head roll to the side, gives me a rueful half smile. "For the present moment, the jury's still out."

"Thanks," I reply, layering the word deep with sarcasm so he won't know how off-balance this conversation has me. Then, because I can't help myself, "You hated me because I'm brave?"

His smile is gone now and he doesn't look away from the wall. "No. I admire you because you're brave. I hated you because…" He opens his hands, searching for words. "Three weeks ago you lost your mom," he says finally, "and I lost everything. *Everything,* Camryn. You have a body. People who love you. Memories. All I have is you."

All he has is me. And…until tonight, I did nothing but ignore him. Call him a hallucination. Refuse to talk to him or even look at him, much less help him figure out what he is.

No wonder he hated me.

I swallow and turn to face the shelves, not quite sure how to feel. "If—if it helps, I've always believed it's choices that make a person who they are. And you still have at least a few of those, even if you don't have…other things." I wave a hand in his direction, but when I pull my gaze from the wall I realize my fingers have gone halfway through his cheek without my noticing.

I don't move. For just a second, barely long enough for

it to register as a thought, I wonder what it would be like to actually touch him. To feel that barest hint of stubble on his jawline. To smooth away that worry line on his forehead.

He looks down. Something strange and sad flits across his face in the moment before he shutters his expression again.

I drop my hand, flushing, my pulse jumping. We both look away.

"Yeah," he says, his tone unreadable, and together we wait in silence until the janitor's whistling is gone.

CHAPTER TWELVE

WHEN I STEP BACK OUT into the hall, the tile is cold and slick against my feet and my teeth start chattering immediately. I'll be lucky if I don't die from pneumonia once all this is over. Unless I can miraculously heal from that too.

I grit my teeth. Two hallways down and one floor up; I'm so close to my answers I can taste it.

I creep around corners, slipping past the rows of silent offices, rerouting whenever I come across a door with light still seeping around its edges. Getting caught by a late-working agent would be almost as bad as running into the blackmailer. At least I don't have to worry about security cameras, though. The agency hasn't had time yet to install

all their usual security measures.

I pause at the top of a stairwell, clutching my shoes to my chest. There's office 209: antique brass knob, expensive nameplate, a tidy little window looking out on the hall. This is it. Last chance to back out, to find some safe little bolt-hole where I can wait for someone else to rescue me.

But there isn't anyone else left, so I stuff my anxiety into the back of my mind and step out of the stairwell.

Quint strides to the end of his ten foot leash and ducks his head through the door. "No one home," he announces. I approach with caution and give the knob a twist. It's locked, but once again, I came prepared.

I pull Kyle's ID out and slide it into the latch. How did he jimmy the lock back at the ticket booth? Sometimes I hate that I have such a good memory—like now, when I can remember not only the way he twisted his driver's license in the lock but also that tense look on his face, that muttered joke about his misspent youth, the way he didn't even think to check his wallet for his ID when he opened it.

I bite my lip hard and angle the card just right, slip it under the catch, push it to the side...*click*. I nudge the knob with a single finger and the door gapes open.

Quint sidles past to scout ahead. I inch in behind him— the carpet is short and plush beneath my feet, muffling my steps—and wait for my eyes to adjust to the simmering darkness. The ceiling fan is on and a sheer white curtain billows against the window, catching the waning moonlight with every twist. Beyond that, gloom spills across the floor in a tangle of too-still shadows.

I fix my gaze on Quint and order my feet to move.

The shadows shift and resolve into furniture, islands looming in the dark. A white leather couch. A bright red chair. A pile of still-packed boxes. A mahogany desk—holding Dr. Lila's office computer.

Trepidation forgotten, I hurry around the desk and press the power button. The monitor blinks on. I squint into the sudden brightness; it's a lock screen, a password prompt. Moment of truth.

I type in the sequence of letters and numbers and hit enter, praying Dr. Lila has the same password for her desktop as she does for her tablet.

A spinning hourglass. A blank green screen. Come on, come on. Quint hunches over the desk at my side and the bright green light washes him out, making him look even more transparent than usual.

Welcome, Evette Lila. The computer stops buzzing.

I scan the home screen; it looks like she uses this computer way less than the tablet because there's hardly any files saved to it. As long as Quint's external drive idea works, that won't be a problem, but if the tablet is well and truly broken then we'll be right back where we started with nothing to show. I rummage in the drawer for a cord. One end to the tablet, the other to the desktop. I plug them in and hold my breath.

A notification pops up, asking me if I want to access the external drive. I click *yes,* then choose one of the resulting files at random—and it opens.

I stare at the screen. It worked. Our ridiculous, one-in-a-million, doomed-from-the-start idea actually worked.

Quint nods and straightens. "Okay," he says, "great. So from here, what's the—"

I hold up a finger. "Say *plan* to me one more time and you will not like the results." I exhale and bend over the computer. "And for your information, I've already figured this part out. We need to unlock the files so they can be read from anywhere and then email them to my account. Tomorrow morning we can find a library or something and open them from there."

"Good plan," he says. His face is straight but there's traces of a smirk in his voice.

I roll my eyes, then click on a random file in the *medical records* folder and right click for options. *It's a bit of a workaround,* Kyle said in the train station. He wasn't kidding. There's got to be twenty choices here, and none of them say "unlock."

Quint's humor evaporates like it never existed and he leans over the keyboard with an intense expression, stabbing a finger at the screen. "Try *Security.*" I click on it, but no dice. It only offers a list of antivirus software and an option to scan the drive.

I glance at the door. How long do we have till the janitor gets to this floor? If we can't figure out how to unlock the info, we'll have no choice but to speed-read as much as we can right here and pray we don't get caught.

"Network options?" Quint suggests.

I double click on the tab as directed and there it is, in tiny red font at the bottom of the screen. *Allow users to access from outside the network.*

Mouth dry, I click the checkbox.

The computer chirps. *File unlocked.*

Jackpot.

Quint and I stare at each other. The moment stretches between us like taffy in the sun: we did it. No more secrets. No more begging for information. No more being one step behind.

A grin spreads over my face. Quint smiles back—then his gaze slips to the computer and the smile melts away, his brow crinkling. He opens his mouth.

Ding! Down the hall, the elevator slides open to tuneless whistling. A mop slaps against the tile.

My hand flies to the mouse. "Is he coming this way?" I hiss to Quint. The window to the hall has no curtains. If the janitor spots the screen's glow, he'll investigate. If he investigates, we're as good as caught.

Quint is across the room with his head through the wall. "We'll have to make a run for it," he calls, voice tight. "He's headed straight for us. Twenty seconds."

I clutch the mouse. How many files can I unlock in twenty seconds? I hover between *Medical records* and *Special projects*—no time to figure out which documents are about Mom and Quint, I'll have to unlock at random and hope for the best. *Click*, options, *click*, network options, *click,* unlock. Again. Again.

Project Sigma. Is that important? Unlock one file there and move to the next. *The Incident,* that's what they call the base explosion. Risk the time to unlock a file there, then on to session logs.

My throat tightens with every choice. All the files I'm leaving behind, all the answers I don't have time to open—I should've been quicker. I should've come up with a better plan.

"He's turned around to put his mop away, let's go!" Quint calls from the doorway.

One more file. One more. I lean in, huddling over the computer. *Click, click, click.* I open a browser, frantically type in my email address, attach the files.

Quint takes two long steps toward me. "Leave it and run!"

I hit send, log out, stuff the tablet beneath the desk and snatch up my shoes—but I only make it three steps into the hall before the janitor spots me.

He drops the mop, pulls his headphones off, and straightens. "Hey! You can't be in there!"

I take off. My bare feet slip on the floor as I skid around the corner. I search for stairs, an elevator, an open window, anything, but it's just another row of locked offices and the janitor's heavy footfalls are way too close already.

"Left!" Quint shouts, and I take the turn blindly. It's a bathroom, a smaller private one with—oh thank God—a locking door. I throw myself inside and flip the bolt. The janitor pounds into the door half a second later and it flexes under the assault. Breathing hard, I back away and search for an exit.

Nothing. No windows, no other doors, not even a person-sized vent.

Quint throws his hands in the air. "I meant 'left at the next hallway, where there's a stairwell,' not 'left, the tiny bathroom with no alternate escape route!'"

"Well you should've been more specific!" I shout back.

"What?" says the janitor, muffled by the door.

"Go away!" I yell at him. My voice cracks and I huddle into myself. Trapped. I'm trapped by the agency again. The panic starts low in my gut and I swallow a whimper, trying to beat it back down. I will *not* have an attack. I can't afford one, not here, not now. Come on, stupid brain, work with me.

The pounding stops. "That's it, I'm calling the cops."

"No!" I yelp, jerking upright. There's no way the police—or Dr. Lila, for that matter—will let me off this time. Maybe if I come up with some sort of convincing, less incriminating story, the janitor will have mercy and let me go.

A plan takes shape. I press my forehead hard against the door and the pain grounds me, letting me squash the panic into a manageable background hum. "Wait a second! I'm coming out, okay?"

"Okay," the janitor says, his bass voice rumbling through the thin door. "Come out, then."

I slide my sneakers on one by one, giving myself plenty of time to think of another option that has even a slightly smaller chance of ending in my arrest, but nothing comes to mind. I take a deep breath and glance at Quint, who shakes his head and says nothing. Then, with trembling fingers, I unlock the bolt and step into the hall.

The janitor crosses his arms and glares at me. He's got his baseball cap clutched in one hand and he's still panting from his run, his bushy mustache bristling with each breath. He eyes me up and down. "How did you get in here?" he demands, stabbing a finger at me. "What were you doing? And don't try to say you were lost, 'cause lost people don't run."

I clear my throat. Here goes. "I was going to...uh, do graffiti."

Quint rubs his temple. "You are seriously the worst criminal ever."

The janitor raises an eyebrow, equally skeptical. "You were gonna do graffiti."

I nod.

"Where's your paint?"

"I dropped it down the trash chute." *Please let there be a trash chute.*

His lips twitch. Time to sell it. What was it Kyle used to tell me about how he always got away with stuff? *A touch of the truth makes a lie easier to swallow.*

I raise my chin and look him in the eye. "My mother was an agency researcher. She died at the base." The words roil in my stomach like acid but I force them out anyway. "And now they won't tell us what happened or even what projects she was working on. They won't listen and I...I wanted to make them answer me, make them *see* me. That's all. I'm sorry. Please don't call the cops."

His rubs his moustache, eyes narrowed. I look at Quint. He holds my gaze, keeping me steady while the janitor considers my words.

"Two of my cousins died at the base too," he tells me,

his voice gruff. "Half the city lost someone. You don't see everyone else out tagging offices, making some underpaid custodian clean up their mess." He digs in his pocket and comes up with a cell phone and I tense to run, but instead of dialing 911, he holds it out to me. "I'll make you a deal. You call someone—a *responsible adult*—to come get you. Everyone goes home, you forget about 'doing graffiti,' you don't get in trouble with the cops and I don't get in trouble with my boss for letting a tagger sneak in. Okay?"

I take the phone gingerly, buying myself time to think. It's a fair offer…but who am I supposed to call? I already tried Dad and Kyle's work phone, and my grandparents live out of state.

I only know one other number. Slowly, I dial it.

It rings twice, because Dad can't bear to disconnect it. I stare at the floor and count my heartbeats and brace myself.

Voicemail picks up. The janitor motions at me to put it on speakerphone and I obey, holding the phone out between us.

"You've reached Marianne Kingfisher," says the voice on the other end, and suddenly I can't breathe. I'm at the base; I'm standing at the gate and talking to my mother and she's alive and helping me and I have a life, I have a family, I have a future. "Leave me a message and I'll call you back. Unless I don't. In which case, just text me." *Beep.*

And she's gone again.

The seconds stretch out. The janitor is staring at me and

I need to say something before he gets suspicious, but I can barely manage to inhale.

"Camryn," Quint says gently, and it's enough to jar me into action.

"Hi," I croak out at last. "It's…me. Um, I need you to come pick me up when you get this. I'm at the temporary agency offices on the east side." My throat closes up, and I know I'm talking to a ghost, but I say it anyway: "I love you."

The janitor grabs the phone. "And she's in some serious trouble too, so I'd appreciate you getting here as soon as possible so I don't have to call the police. Thanks." He hangs up and looks at me. "Who was that, your aunt or something?"

"Yeah," I lie. My eyes are stinging, but hopefully he'll think I'm only emotional about getting caught. I clear my throat. "I'll wait for her outside."

Actually, I'll run like hell the second I hit fresh air, but he doesn't need to know that yet.

"Good thinking," Quint says. I don't meet his eyes though, because I know what he'd look like to me at this moment: rubble and ash, soot and silence, force and fire. But now, now that he's become—what? An ally? A frenemy?—the thought of seeing him that way again, as a representation of what I've lost…it's suddenly unbearable. So, eyes firmly fixed on the corridor, I scoot past and pray the janitor buys my story.

No luck. His beefy hand closes around my shoulder before I get two steps. "We'll wait right here," he says, eyes narrowed.

I swallow. With no other option, I stand still and wait for him to realize I'm lying.

The minutes tick by. Every time he checks his silent phone, my blood pressure goes up a few more notches. No one's going to call and no one's going to come. Sooner or later, he's either going to have to let me go or call the cops.

At the ten minute mark he makes his decision. "Time's up, kid. Either your aunt's asleep or you're lying." He thumbs his phone on and starts dialing 911.

A few years ago, Kyle gave me a very short but effective lesson in self-defense. This feels like the right time to test it out.

I take a long step sideways, whirl around, and knee the janitor hard in the crotch.

He folds in on himself like a house of cards and I dart down the hall, wincing in sympathy. Hopefully I've bought myself enough time for a clean getaway, because part two of Kyle's lesson made it clear that if this guy catches up with me he's not going to be in a forgiving mood.

I tear around the corner and nearly trip over the abandoned mop bucket, losing several precious seconds while I regain my footing. An incensed bellow ricochets off the walls behind me. My head start is over.

"Stairs, stairs!" Quint shouts, and I veer to the right and

bound down the steps three at a time—but instead of taking me to a first floor landing, they end in a brown door with a bright red bar across it. EMERGENCY EXIT ONLY, it says. *Alarm will sound.* It's a little late to worry about stealth, so I plow into it at full speed and stumble out onto a sidewalk. The fire alarm's shrill screech heralds my exit and I cringe, covering my ears.

The movement costs me a second too long. A brawny hand snaps shut around my wrist and the janitor hauls me back toward the door, his face red and twisted with pain. Ice shoots through my veins and pools in my stomach. Once he turns me over to the cops, I'm done for. I try to wrench my arm away, but his grip is ironclad and a row of tall bushes separate me from the street, from anyone who might see and help. He twists hard, and I'm up on my tiptoes, trying to catch my breath, trying frantically to think of a way out of this—

—and then there's a low, electric buzz, and the janitor freezes. His hand tightens and releases, tightens and releases, a spasm that nearly jerks my arm out of its socket. I cry out and finally manage to pull away, landing hard on the sidewalk. I stare up at him, spellbound, as his spine arcs and his face tilts upward like a drowning man straining for the surface.

Then he lets out a long breath and sags, swaying. In the

second before he hits the ground he lowers his eyes to meet mine and something is…

Wrong. Missing.

Just like the trainmaster.

He crumbles to the sidewalk, twitching like a fresh-caught fish. I'm sitting, staring, breathless—so it takes me longer than it should to see the person who was standing behind him.

The gun slides out of the shadows first.

Time slows down and pulls apart, spreading the moment like dough under a rolling pin. The weapon is modified, something out of a steampunk show: gleaming silver wires twine around the barrel and meet at the handle, which is fashioned from a chunk of the same shimmery metal. The weapon is clunky, heavy, but the hand that holds it isn't shaking.

The hand is followed by a hoodie sleeve: black, wrinkled. The sleeve is followed by an arm, and the arm is followed by a boy.

Ash blond hair falling over his glasses. Bright green eyes hooded by shadows. No lab coat. And no transparency.

The gun lowers. "It's about time," says the solid version of Quint. "I've been looking for you everywhere."

CHAPTER THIRTEEN

U NABLE TO PROCESS THE SCENE as a whole, my mind breaks it into fragments.

The solid-looking Quint, reaching down to help me up. I flinch away, because I'm terrified his hand will go right through mine and terrified it won't.

My see-through Quint a few yards away, silent as the stillness at the center of the universe. His lab coat is a splash of brilliance against the shadows, and it makes me think of the too-bright paint behind my family portrait: an afterimage, just a false-color remnant of life.

The janitor, twitching and gasping on the concrete as if he's been electrified. His eyes are rolled up in his head, but I can still see that awful *emptiness*.

They're empty because he's dying. And he's dying because someone shot him.

I scrabble backwards on the sidewalk. The solid Quint is still standing in front of the janitor, free hand held out to help me up. "I'm sorry about your brother," he says. "I didn't intend that kind of collateral damage."

And this is how my blackmailer chooses to introduce himself. Not with a name. With an apology. With a gleaming quicksilver gun that I've seen once before, bright and blurry in a snapshot of his hoodie pocket. With a too-familiar frown pulling at one corner of his mouth as his hand touches mine—warm, solid, *wrong*—and closes around it, and tightens, and pulls me to my feet.

My lips are tingling and my hands feel clammy and my thoughts are tumbling and slippery. I've been through too many impossible things tonight and my brain is putting on the brakes. But there is one thing I know: I know how to read Quint's expressions, and right now they're showcased on this strange boy's face. He's apologizing for his bomb's "collateral damage" while ignoring the dying man right behind him—and I think he means it. I think he is sorry. And I think he'd do it again.

Fury pounds through my veins, hard and dark, energizing and sickening and potent. I want him to hurt. I want him to pay. I want him to *understand*.

I snatch my hand from his. I back away.

The janitor is still twitching on the sidewalk. Beneath the wailing fire alarm, his fingernails scrape a spastic rhythm against the concrete, reminding me that I should be starting CPR, I should be looking for help, I should be trying to save him. But I tried to save the trainmaster, and I failed. Because it was a trap.

"How did you find me?" I demand. I'm still moving away, putting space between us, terrified and tempted by the rage that's shrieking through me. A few hours ago I punched a man just because he called my mom a terrorist bitch. If I don't control myself right now, what will I do to my brother's murderer?

I know what I *want* to do.

I clench my hands. Unclench them. If I can distract him long enough, someone will come, someone will see, someone will arrest him. They'll arrest me too, but I don't think I care anymore.

The solid Quint is preoccupied, leaning sideways to glance at the street beyond the bushes. "I traced the calls to your parents' phones. Look, we'll play twenty questions later. We're about to get tossed in jail in approximately three minutes, and we should probably spend that time running for our lives. Come on."

"Like hell I'm going anywhere with you," I spit out.

But, oh God, he looks just like my Quint, reaching out to me with that exasperated look on his face—and my damn instincts run in circles, telling me *trust him* and *run* and *make him pay, make him pay, make him pay.*

He takes a step closer. "You're looking for answers," he says. "I can give them to you. But we have to go *now*."

Layered beneath the still-screeching fire alarm, a new siren takes up the call. Cops are headed this way, and through the hedge I can already make out people spilling onto the sidewalks to see what's going on. My fingernails dig into my palms with the effort of staying put—I have to hold on just a little longer. "Who are you?"

He throws out his arms, exasperated. "Dr. Matthew Lerato, okay? And you're Camryn Kingfisher. Can we run away now or are there any more pleasantries you'd like to exchange while we wait for the police?"

The fury roars and thunders, making my hands shake. "You killed my brother, you son of a *bitch,* and now you want—"

"Not exactly," he cuts in.

"What?"

"Your brother. He's not exactly dead."

And just like that the world closes in around me. No more sirens, no more fire alarm. Only me and Dr. Matthew Lerato, murderer, who says my brother isn't exactly dead.

I stop backing away. The rage mixes with a frantic sort of hope, the kind I know is almost certainly false but can't help reaching for anyway.

Unable to stop myself, I look at Quint.

He catches my eye. Takes a breath. He opens his mouth—and nothing comes out. His face is blank, shocked. Terrified.

I'm on my own. I turn back to Matthew, hesitate, clench and unclench my hands again. "What the hell is that supposed to mean?" I say at last.

"It means I know what's happening to you. And I can tell you—if you come with me, right *now*."

The sirens are almost upon us. My maybe-hallucination can't help me, and Kyle might not be dead, and this boy who I almost know says he has the answers I've been desperate for.

I take a step forward.

"No," Quint says. My gaze jerks to him. He's still unmoving, still terrified, but now he's focused on me and there's something dark and jagged in his voice. "Don't trust him," he tells me. "Run."

But the hope pulls and tugs and burns and it's so much more powerful and so much more painful than the fury. "Somewhere public," I tell Matthew before I can stop myself.

He's headed for the street already, stuffing his gun back in his pocket. "Fine. Where?" he calls over his shoulder.

I hesitate. The janitor's nails have stopped scraping against the concrete. Someone is shouting just around the corner—one of the agents who was working late, probably—and flashing police lights are reflecting blue and red off the buildings at the end of the block. All I'd need to do is wait a few more seconds, and Matthew would be caught.

I square my shoulders, stride forward, and grab his arm. "Follow me."

———

The Pie Hole is a 24-hour truck stop tucked away beneath an overpass, permanently guarded by a cadre of homeless people and stray dogs. The vinyl seats are cracked, the jukebox only plays '80s pop, and the ceiling rattles every time a truck hits the on-ramp—but the familiar smell of tart cherries and flaky crust and creamy meringue wrap tight around me like a childhood quilt, and for this conversation, I'm going to need that.

"You have twenty minutes before I decide whether to turn you in," I tell Matthew flatly as soon as the waitress seats us.

Quint is sitting next to him, head bowed over the table, hands buried in his hair, silent, still. He didn't look at either of us during the half-mile jog from the agency office, and he hasn't moved since we sat down. I can't blame him. I can barely look at him, either. If Matthew is the blackmailer, then who is this shadow I've been tied to for three weeks?

"We'll be done in ten," Matthew says. His gaze slides to the red-eyed truckers in the booth opposite ours, and he lowers his voice. "After that, I'd be screwed anyway. They can track me if I stay out too long."

"Who can track you?" I keep my voice level and my posture rigid. Ask questions, get answers. That's all I'm here for.

He scowls, like it should be obvious. "The agency."

"Why is the agency tracking you?"

He takes off his glasses and sighs, cleaning them on the edge of his hoodie. The motion is unnervingly familiar. "It's a long story, and I'm betting you'd rather spend our ten minutes on your own issues."

I put my fisted hands on the table and lean forward. "Like why you tried to kill me? It was you who set the bomb, wasn't it?" I struggle to keep my voice down. Ask questions, get answers. Focus.

He slides his glasses back on. "That was before I had all the facts about the situation," he says, "and if you'd been in my position at the time, you'd have done the same thing."

A vision flashes through my mind: a trainmaster with empty eyes, there one moment and gone the next. Unnerved, I shake it away. "Never," I snarl. "I would *never.*"

His lips thin out. "Not killing is easy when you never have to make a choice."

The waitress approaches with our orders and we're forced into silence. It seethes with the things he's said and I want to leave, want to hurt him, want to go someplace where I can breathe, but—not yet. Not until I get what I came for.

The pie plates clatter to the table. My order is a slice of cherry rhubarb, and I take a bite to keep myself quiet until the waitress moves out of earshot. Matthew follows suit and then makes a face. "This is awful," he says. The waitress doesn't even bother to give him a dirty look.

I take another bite. "Yeah, the apple is the only good kind here," I reply, in what I hope is a normal voice.

Matthew motions at my cherry rhubarb. "Then why didn't you get it?"

I push the pie away. The waitress is out of range now and I won't waste time on chitchat. "I want to know what was on the tablet. And I want to know about Kyle." I try to tamp down the hope but it leaks into my voice anyway.

He smiles a strange little smile, half sad, half resigned. "You'll know soon enough." He taps his fork against his plate. "But you have another problem—when you woke up after the bomb, a few things were different about the city, right?"

I narrow my eyes but allow him to temporarily sidetrack me, because I need these answers too. "My apartment was empty and the streets were dry. And there was no evidence of your attempt at mass murder."

A wall of force and fire. I don't shake the memory off this time. It grounds me, keeps me aware of who I'm with and what he's done and how very unsafe I am.

At Matthew's side, Quint drops his hands to the table. He lays them flat, pauses like he's gathering his strength, and lifts his head. His gaze is still carefully trained on the middle distance and not on either of us, but he's listening.

Matthew nods. "That's because you weren't in the same place anymore. After the bomb, you shifted to an alternate timeline."

Quint inhales. He closes his eyes like he's in pain.

"Explain," I demand.

Matthew checks his watch and his expression tightens a few notches. "An alternate timeline is a kind of parallel reality: several versions of the same world existing in side-by-side dimensions, mostly the same, but with some minor deviations that can have a ripple effect—"

"I watch sci-fi, I *know* what an alternate timeline is," I hiss. I'm gripping the edge of the table now and it's splintering beneath my nails, but I don't let go. Ask questions, get answers. Ask questions, get answers. "How could I have switched to a different timeline? And why should I believe anything you say?"

Matthew's words are clipped. "My best guess is that the life-or-death scenario triggered your abilities. The bomb went off and then you shifted yourself here." He leans forward. "And you should believe what I say, Camryn King-fisher, because you have no other options, and because I'm telling the truth, and because I need you."

A waitress brushes by on her way to a neighboring table. The silence simmers until she's out of range. "For what?" I demand once she's returned to the kitchen. "And what do you mean by my *abilities*?"

But Matthew shakes his head. "Later. There's something else you need to know, right? You keep glancing at a spot next to me. Almost like there's someone else here."

Quint's gaze jerks to mine. The connection is a jolt of electricity, a conduit, and the only thing flowing through it is fear. He wants me to run. He doesn't want to hear whatever Matthew will say next, and he doesn't want me to hear it either. But I need this information. I know I can't trust its source, but right now my choices are limited. "Yes," I manage. "Quint."

"He's me." It's not a question.

My mouth is dry. It takes me two tries to speak. "Why do I see you?"

A pair of truckers pass by, grumbling, and Matthew waits until they're gone to answer. "Because in your time-line, I'm dead."

Quint's eyes go flat, icy and eerie: too calm. He doesn't move.

"Why am I the only one who can see him?" It's getting harder to speak, harder to tell whether my voice is too loud. He's giving me my answers and now I'm drowning in them.

Matthew leans forward, puts his hands flat on the table, and nods. "That," he says, "is the right question."

Another trucker shuffles toward the exit, a sour expression on her face. At a table a few yards away, a waitress is bent down, saying something in a low voice to the tired-looking family seated there. The mom's lips purse and her eyes go wide, and she scoops up her baby without a word and heads for the exit.

I blink. A few minutes ago, The Pie Hole was full and busy. Now, the last trickle of customers is headed for the door and the jukebox is crooning '80s rock ballads to an empty room.

When I look back, Matthew's hands aren't on the table anymore. "I should've said eight minutes," he says lightly, but he's wearing that strange smile again, sad and resigned.

I open my mouth but before I can say anything, the cushion on my bench dips, announcing that someone has sat down next to me. I scoot away and turn to tell the stranger that the booth is taken—and then I go still.

"I miss the days when I was the only one getting in trouble at three o'clock in the morning," Kyle says, and folds his hands atop the table.

Deep in some dark, murky place inside my soul, I knew that my brother was dead. *Knew* it, no matter what Matthew said. The familiar agony of it has been shifting and cracking inside me for hours like the plates beneath the earth. So when I see him, wonderfully but utterly *impossibly* alive, the fissures grind and rumble and gape because—

Something is off.

It takes me a few seconds to place it.

———

"Hi, Dr. Lerato," Kyle says. His voice is level and his smile is easy, but there's violence in his eyes and he still hasn't looked at me. "The agency sends you greetings, in the form of a few dozen heavily-armed gunmen surrounding this building. Though as the designated negotiator, I, of course, am unarmed, in case you were wondering."

"Your source told you to come alone," Matthew replies. His hands are still under the table.

My brother tilts his head. "I never do as I'm told. Now. Put your gun away and let my sister go or I'll kill you."

Matthew raises his brow. "You said you were unarmed. You're hardly in a position to make personal threats."

Kyle smiles his sharp-edged smile. "I didn't say I would kill you with a gun."

———

Their hands. That's what's wrong.

Matthew's hands are still under the table—because he's got his gun out, most likely. But more important are Kyle's hands. They're clasped together in a white-knuckled grip, rough and callused, darkened by oil around the nails because he works on his bike in his free time.

But not bandaged. Not bloody, not scraped raw.

A rusted wheel dripping with blood.

Not scorched, not injured, not blown to pieces.

A wall of force and fire.

Alternate timeline. Not *my* timeline.

Not my Kyle.

And not exactly dead.

———

Matthew's gaze shifts to me. "If you get away, come find me. I'll tell you what was on the tablet." He closes his eyes.

Kyle leaps out of his seat. Too slow.

Matthew lifts his hands. In one is his steampunk stun gun, aimed at me. In the other is a palm-sized metal orb. He drops it.

It hits the vinyl with a tinny rattle and explodes into a supernova.

The world flares into brilliance. The light curls through my brain, burns me and blinds me. Glass shatters. Gunshot. Quint cries out my name.

Someone is hunched over me, shielding me with his body. He smells like expensive aftershave and forty-weight oil. Not my Kyle, but still my Kyle.

The light fades. From under my brother's arm, I squint at the table. Matthew is gone. Our forgotten pies are skewered with broken glass from the window, and the cherry sauce in mine shines against the shards like bright blood. Mom would've hated that. Cherry rhubarb was her favorite order.

Beneath the booth, Kyle's hand is splayed on the ground atop a sleek black gun.

I look from it to the broken window. "I thought you were unarmed," I say. My voice is distant and dreamlike in my own ears—an aftereffect of the light bomb, or my own shock?

Kyle doesn't answer. I push out from beneath him, and he rolls lifelessly off.

My breath stutters and I'm on my knees, leaned over him, checking his pulse with shaking fingers—but he's alive, his heartbeat drumming steady and strong, his eyes open but unresponsive.

I grip the edge of the table and leverage myself to my feet. Glass shards bite into my fingers, but I ignore the pain, because throughout the whole restaurant, everyone is frozen. A waitress is stopped midstride two booths over, her head turned and her mouth half open. The last trucker is staring blankly into the parking lot. The cashier is reaching for a button on the register, his finger hovering inches away, unmoving.

I step past my brother. Past the cashier and the trucker, empty-eyed dolls in a silent museum. Through the front door. Into the midnight air that drapes around my shoulders, warm and pie scented.

On the street out front, on the interstate overhead, cars are stopped. Three or four have collided and their drivers are slouched over inflated airbags. The rest of the vehicles are gliding to a halt on curbs and sidewalks and in the middle of the street, and in their seats people are gripping steering wheels and staring at nothing. A block away, tires screech as cars with conscious drivers try to navigate the cluttered road.

Paralyzed. Everyone within sight of the light bomb has been paralyzed, except me. And, apparently, Matthew.

What about the heavily armed gunmen? How long will their paralysis last, and what will they do with me when they wake up?

If you get away, Matthew said.

My brother's bike is leaned up against the restaurant wall, helmet dangling from the handlebars, key in the ignition. I can sense Quint behind me as I stride toward it, but I'm not ready to look at him yet. Heart racing, I shove the helmet over my head, then sling myself onto the glossy black machine and start the engine.

I pause. Swallow. Stare back through the broken front

window at the skewered pies, and think about expensive aftershave and forty-weight oil.

Quint has already climbed on behind me. He leans forward over my shoulder and turns his head: icy, eerie, too calm. I've spent so long trying to figure out who and what he is, and now that I know I want to take it all back.

"Run," he tells me.

And this time, I listen.

———

When I'm ten miles away, I stop and call Kyle from a pay phone.

This time he picks up. "You do remember you failed your road test." His voice is unsteady, flat, and tightly wound—but I soak it up like rain in the desert because my brother is okay. My brother is okay, my brother is alive, and I don't care which version of him it is because he's not dead and it's not my fault and for the first time in hours I can finally breathe again.

"Risk I had to take," I reply when I'm sure the words will come out smooth. Then, because I've been fleeing for fifteen minutes with no sign of pursuit: "You said we were surrounded."

"I also said I knew how to kill someone without a gun."

I'm silent.

"I'm an analyst," he says after a moment, still with that odd tight shakiness. "I barely know how to kill someone *with* a gun. The agency would've never let me near that negotiation, if they even bothered to negotiate at all."

I close my eyes and sag against the phone booth. *Your source told you to come alone,* Matthew said. And he had. For me? "You were bluffing."

"And you were dead."

My eyes snap open and I steady myself with a hand against the booth's wall. "What?"

"What the hell are you *doing,* Cam? The last three weeks you just let us think you got blown up at the base along with everyone else and now I find out you've been running around with a terrorist the whole time? How could you let *him* be the one to tell me you were alive, to set up whatever the hell kind of meeting that was? Do you know what we went through after you and Mom...Didn't you think about what Dad—what I—" He cuts off, and for a second there's only breathing.

"Kyle?" My voice is barely a whisper. I'm dead. In this timeline, the other version of me is dead and gone, ashes and rubble. I've been mourning my brother for hours, and he's been mourning me for weeks.

And also: Matthew is a terrorist.

There's shouting in the background. Kyle's voice lowers.

"Look. Wherever you're going, get there fast and get there safe, before my bosses figure out I held back vital intelligence to save my kid sister." The line goes dead.

I drop the phone. When I ride away it's still dangling, beeping out a busy tone, begging for another quarter.

CHAPTER FOURTEEN

T HE THIRD TIME I CRASH the bike, I can't force myself to climb back on.

I sit at the lip of the ditch and stare down at it: side pipes hissing in the mud, wheels spinning in the air, belly up like a dead goldfish. None of the crashes have been major, but I'm too exhausted and unskilled to push myself any further tonight. There's an abandoned barn on the horizon and it looks like as good a place as any to catch a few hours of sleep before I...

Before I do what?

I sneak a glance at Quint. He's standing a few feet away with his hands in his pockets and the moonrise gleaming through his torso, not looking at me in the same way he's been not looking at me for the last hour.

It's torture, being stuck with him. The emotion has been churning inside me, growing with every minute, every mile. I hate who he is, hate what the other version of him has done to me—and at the same time I feel so terribly, impossibly *cheated*. Because that boy from an hour ago, the mysterious maybe-hallucination who I could talk to and was maybe even starting to like a little, he's gone forever. I despise myself for missing him, and I despise Matthew for taking him away from me, and I despise not knowing how to stop feeling things I shouldn't feel about people who aren't even alive.

It's all an ugly, snarled mess in my head, and it makes me want to hurt someone.

"So," I say to Quint, trudging into the ditch to retrieve the bike, "remember anything yet about your psychopathic former life?" The words are cruel and hard and I hate that they feel wrong even as they leave my mouth. I should *want* to hurt him. Where's that awful anger now, when it would actually be justified?

"No," he says quietly, still looking at the moon.

"How do I know you're not lying?"

"You don't."

"Then what good are you?" I demand, and the words burn like acid. I turn my back and let them eat at both of us as I kneel down and use my sleeve to wipe mud off the seat. The bike looks okay. A few more dents than it had at The Pie Hole, maybe, but from what Kyle said on the phone he's got bigger problems than bike repairs anyway.

I shove the motorcycle up the side of the ditch with more force than necessary, and it flops to the grass. I pull myself up after it and brush at the mud on my pants before I give up the venture as pointless. I heave the bike upright and take a breath, trying to re-center myself, trying to focus on figuring out our next step.

My. My next step.

"If...if you could remember anything about being him," I start, trying to keep my voice level, but he cuts me off.

"I'm not him." There's acid in his voice now too. He's turned toward me a little, moonlight glinting off his glasses.

I shove the bike forward. "Tomorrow morning I'm going to the library to read the files we unlocked," I say, "and I'm also going to look up some information on your evil twin. If there's anything of interest you can tell me about the two of you first, it *might* help convince me I can trust you at least a little. Otherwise, I can just go back to completely ignoring you again."

He stares at me like I've punched him. It's the worst thing I could threaten him with, the only thing he has left—my acknowledgement of his existence. "Now who's manipulating who?" he says, and I block the surge of shame, because damn it, *he's* the bad guy here. I've got to find out what was on that tablet and whether it proves Mom's innocence, have to figure out how to stop Matthew from whatever he might do to hurt me or my family next, and in the meantime Quint is nothing but a liability.

I grit my teeth. "I am stuck in some alternate timeline—"

"According to *him*."

"—with no clue how I got here and no clue what my *abilities* might do next, and he's the only one who seems to know anything about any of it. And once the agency figures out what happened at The Pie Hole, they're going to assume I'm in league with a terrorist," the word leaves a bitter taste in my mouth, "the same way Kyle did. So you can either help me find him and figure all of this out, or we can go back to the way things were between us a few days ago."

He stops and I do too. He steps in close, leans down. I remember how he looked at the fountain: green eyes like cut glass, and if I met his gaze it would slice me open.

I look away.

He doesn't. "I know you need to know what happened with your Mom, but do you really think you can trust anything he'd tell you?"

"No." Some of the venom has leeched out of my voice because I can't sustain it, not with him looking at me like that. "But I need to know what he knows. What other choice do I have?"

"Run," he says, without hesitation. "Run, and keep on running, and don't look back."

I push the bike forward again and he steps out of the way right before I walk through him. "I've done nothing but run lately," I reply. "Run from my fears, hide from the truth, give up when things go wrong. And you know what? None of it helps. It's never helped. I'm done running." My shoulders slump. Mom would say this realization is a break-through, but I just feel tired, and afraid, and so, so alone.

Quint keeps pace at my side, lab coat billowing like a storm cloud. "Okay, fine, but you can't go to *him*. There's got to be another option."

"I already told you the other option. Remember something, and help me."

His eyes darken. He walks a little faster. "No."

"That's it? Just no?"

"I told you I couldn't remember anything," he snaps over his shoulder.

"I don't want you to," I tell him, because it's true. I don't know if people are more than the sum of their memories, but if his come back, it'll mean he's that much closer to being Dr. Matthew Lerato and that much further from being the maybe-hallucination I had an *our* with. "But you could think of something that can help us. You and him were different versions of the same person, right? You have to have some of the same knowledge. So maybe if you really tried, you could at least remember something about alternate timelines and how I could've jumped into one."

"I don't know anything about that." His jaw is tight, the words clipped.

"What about—"

He explodes. "I *don't know*!" he shouts, whirling on me. "I don't have his memories, because I'm not him! I'm *not*, okay? Please, Camryn, please believe me, because if you don't, I'm not sure I can either."

We stare at each other for a long moment—then he inhales, spins around, and takes three wide strides before he jerks to a stop like a marionette with its strings caught. He doesn't move, muscles bunched up like he's pushing at a wall.

I swallow. "Quint," I say, but then falter.

He rakes a hand through his hair with a jerky motion and then, after a moment, his shoulders sag. When he turns around, his eyes are bright and shining and I feel like an intruder. He takes a deep breath. "Did you know," he says with a bitter, painful sort of smile, "that the furthest I can go from you is exactly ten feet and three inches? I've tested it a thousand times. I know it by heart. But every once in a while, I try to escape from you again anyway. And I can never get far enough."

The words drift down, settle to the ground between us. They spread like molasses, slow and heavy, until the silence is too much.

He closes his eyes and bows his head, blowing out a long breath. The crickets chirp all around us and somewhere in the distance an owl hoots, but I stay quiet. I wait for him to say whatever it is that has him so scared, because I've done enough running of my own to understand that it's not only me he's trying to escape from.

"There's something there," he says at last, head still bowed. "In my past. In his past. Every time I looked at him I could feel it. And I think it's something personal and important and *terrible*, but I can't remember it, and I'm starting to think it's because I don't want to. Please, Camryn. Please don't make me remember it."

He's asking me to save him. To separate him. To trust him. And that feels like the worst decision I could possibly make… but I think not making it might hurt me as much as him.

My hands curl around the handlebars of my brother's bike tight enough to make my fingers ache. I take a deep breath—and then let go. The bike sags against a tree as I turn to face Quint. "A few hours ago, there were two versions of you at that train station. One who bombed it and murdered at least three people."

His shoulders rise and fall with a breath. He stays silent, waiting for my judgment.

"And…another one who was afraid of the dark, and who said he might not like himself if he knew who he was, and who kept me moving until I made it to the surface."

I make myself look at him, make myself hold his gaze when he lifts his head. It's not as hard as it was a moment ago. I think now, maybe I might be the one who could slice him open.

I take a step closer. "When we were in that janitor's closet, you told me you used to hate me because of all the things I had that you didn't. I told you I believed it was choices that make a person who they are. Not their memories, not their past. And—and I'm not sure if I can still believe that, but I want to. God, Quint, I want to. So…this is me, giving you a chance to convince me I was right the first time."

He exhales, closes his eyes, scrubs a hand across his face. "Thank you," he says roughly. When he opens his eyes, the glint of vulnerability is hidden away again and he gives me his old half-smile. "If you don't want to wait till tomorrow to check the files, I think there's a laptop in the saddlebag."

I freeze. "Seriously?" I hiss, torn between anger that he waited so long to tell me and elation that I can get a head start on finding answers.

He lifts one shoulder. The smile stays, but it doesn't reach his eyes anymore. "This is me trying to be convincing," he says simply.

I grab the bike's handlebars again and hurry toward the barn. When we reach it, I rummage through Kyle's bags. My heart thumps hard when I come up with a small, heavy duty computer. I log into a guest account and pull up my email. It's tempting to try and guess my brother's password to see if there are more agency files on here, but the security features might lock me out and alert his higher-ups if I get it wrong.

Then I pause. I glance over my shoulder; Quint is wandering into the barn, ignoring me, a closed-off expression on his face.

I navigate to a search engine and type in Dr. Matthew Lerato.

The Wi-Fi connects to a local 4G network and after a short wait, an array of news articles fills the screen. "Interview with a Teen Physics Genius." "Youngest Doctoral Candidate in the State Wins National Prize." "Prodigy Joins Army's New Research Branch."

There's a picture. Lab coat, green eyes, half smile.

He's standing next to Dr. Lila. And he's shaking hands with my mother.

I hit the exit button as fast as my fingers can move and sit there, staring at a blank blue background, unable to breathe.

Mom didn't know. She was welcoming a new recruit. She didn't know who he was, what he'd do to Kyle, what he'd do to me. This doesn't mean the two of them were involved in some kind of agency conspiracy together. It doesn't mean Dr. Lila was right. It doesn't mean anything.

But they'd worked together. She knew him. How could she have known him?

I close my eyes, but the image is burned into my brain. The details rush at me all at once, an avalanche of the things I've tried hardest to forget and remember all at the same time: her long chestnut hair tied in a messy braid and skewered with a chewed-up pencil. A fixed smile on her face because she spent half her life on autopilot while she analyzed research in her head. A Doctor Who T-shirt peeking out from beneath her blue-and-gray jacket because she took every chance she could to rebel against the strict uniform code. And that bracelet. That damn bracelet that she stole, that made me realize I'd never really known her at all.

My eyes burn. I shove the image away and refocus on the other side of the picture—Dr. Lila, smiling at the boy she let me believe didn't exist.

Matthew worked at the agency base. And Matthew is a bomber.

The equation is ugly, full of spikes and snares and things

I don't want to think about. But I just told Quint I was done running, so I open my eyes, log into my email, and open the secrets they've been keeping from me.

I managed to unlock five files. I scroll through them, reading slowly and meticulously, trying to absorb any hint of helpful information. The first document contains one of Dr. Lila's daily logs from about a week ago, but it's annotated in some weird shorthand that I can't make sense of. The next is a departmental memo reminding agents that their confidentiality agreements prohibited them from talking to the press about "the incident," which is what they call the explosion that killed nearly five thousand people. Then come two requisition orders for "Project Sigma," listing a bunch of scientific equipment to be delivered to the south end of the base—the explosion's epicenter.

I grit my teeth. Four files down, and not one of them has told me anything new. With a muttered prayer, I open the last document. It's an X-ray labeled with my name.

Quint's leaning against the wall a few feet away now, glancing at the screen over my shoulder. When he spots the X-ray he pushes off and takes a step closer. "Wait," he says. "I saw that right before you got caught by the janitor. Something's off about it."

I peer at the ghostly black-and-white imagery. I know the basics of reading an X-ray, and he's right. Something's odd here.

He finds it before I do. "Aren't you supposed to have surgical implants?"

"Yeah. Steel screws in my leg and shoulder." The doctors told me they'd been implanted in the days immediately following the accident, when I'd been in a medical coma, but according to this scan they don't exist.

Quint points at the X-ray date; it's from last week. "So if it wasn't the implants that set off the metal detector—and, probably, helped trigger the bomb—what was it?"

I narrow my eyes. I point at the chest, trace my way down the aorta. "Why," I ask, "are my blood vessels giving off metallic signatures?"

This is part of what the agency has been hiding from me, what they must've been covering up when they lied about my implants. The only problem is, I have no idea what it means.

Quint is silent. A frown cuts across his face and he steps away, retreating into the shadows to think or loiter broodingly or whatever it is he does when he's wearing that faraway glower. I close out the useless files and slam the laptop's lid shut.

All the answers I manage to find only bring up more questions.

<hr />

We ditch the bike the next morning. The agency probably knows to look for it by now, and it ran out of fuel a couple miles into town anyway. I wheel it behind a derelict gas station, hide the key atop a tire, and hope Kyle finds it before a thief does.

I think about leaving him a note, but I'm still not sure whose side he'd take if he were forced to choose. Any information I give him could end up helping the agency find me that much quicker.

I clench my hands and stuff them in my pockets. "Do you think he's real?" I ask Quint before I can stop myself.

He glances up. We're picking our way through a seedy back alley, sidestepping trash cans and hissing cats while I try to figure out how to locate Matthew's lair. "I'm not exactly the best judge of who's real and who's not," Quint answers, looking straight ahead.

I keep my eyes on my feet, managing a jerky nod as I step over a moldy takeout container. A man clothed mostly in garbage bags is digging through a dumpster a few yards away and I take a quick right down a different alley so he won't hear me talking to myself. Not that he'd care, I guess.

Quint peers at me, then hesitates a moment before he takes off his glasses with a sigh. "I can't say for sure," he answers, "but based on the similarities to our version of reality, I'd guess this timeline branched off from ours not too long ago. So although this Kyle isn't your Kyle, he only very recently stopped being your Kyle." His tone is determined, like he has to force the words out, and he's scrubbing at his glasses as if his life depends on it.

I feel around the edges of our truce, trying to guess at how much information he can give me without having to remember more than he wants to. "So you think this time-line is close to our timeline."

He's walking ahead of me now, back straight, gaze focused on the distance as I follow at his heels. He takes a right turn out of the alley onto a narrow residential street. I duck my head, hoping none of the passing commuters notice my sewer-chic look and decide to call the cops.

"You've noticed that a few things are different, but have you thought about how many things are the same?" Quint goes on. "Almost everything. There are a lot of theories about parallel realities, but from what—what he said—" he flounders for a second, but then goes on, his tone still stiff, "about ripple effects, I think this timeline must've been artificially created, and I think whatever did it, it happened recently." His tone goes dark. "Someone's been screwing with the universe, and it's not going to end well."

I stare at his back. So that's what this is about. He doesn't feel bad for me because of Kyle, and he's not giving me information out of the goodness of his heart. He's trying to warn me away from Matthew again. And he's not wrong; Matthew apparently has the technology to travel between timelines himself, and he also doesn't seem to have much in the way of ethics, so it wouldn't be a stretch to think he might've been one of the people who helped "screw with the universe" in the first place.

"How can a timeline be artificially created?" I ask flatly.

"The grandfather paradox," he replies, equally flat.

I stop walking, and after a second he's forced to as well. "*Time travel?*" My words echo off the houses that line the street, and I snap my mouth shut when a woman gives me a dirty look from her porch swing—but I've watched enough sci-fi to know what he's talking about. The grandfather paradox is a classic thought experiment that tells the story of a man who goes back in time and winds up accidentally killing his own grandfather, which means the time traveler himself never could've been born, which means he couldn't have gone back in time and killed anyone in the first place. The story is used to illustrate one of the problems that makes time travel pretty much impossible.

"Some theories say that the moment the traveler changes the past by killing his grandfather, an alternate timeline would be created," Quint says, and we start walking again. He stays ahead of me where I can't see his expression. "A parallel reality living right next to the original, but with minor variations caused by the changes. Those changes have a ripple effect: maybe the grandfather was supposed to have invented the Internet, but in that version of reality he got killed too soon so it never gets created. Maybe some other invention takes its place instead, and then the present-day world of that timeline ends up looking completely different from ours—all because a hundred years ago, one man died instead of lived."

"And because the timeline we're in right now doesn't have that many big differences, you think whatever change was made to create it happened recently."

"I would estimate," he says, sliding his glasses back on, "about three weeks ago."

The numbness is slow, creeping through my bones and weighing down my breaths. Three weeks ago. The explosion. The agency. Matthew. Mom. The puzzle pieces jangle against each other, refusing to fit together.

Lost in his thoughts, Quint takes a left turn. This part of town is mostly vacant housing and a few abandoned offices with nothing but stray cats and empty windows to watch me as I stride past. DEAD-END AHEAD, proclaims a yellow sign.

"Camryn," Quint says suddenly, "I know we're not friends, but do you...can you trust me?"

I want to tell him no, because that's what my answer should be, and also because if I say yes he's going to ask me to trust him now and run again—but he'll know if I lie to him, the same way I know when he does. "We've been through several near-death experiences together," I answer at last. "I've stopped ignoring you. Mostly. And you've been a manipulative bastard slightly less than you could've been in the last few hours. If that doesn't make us friends I don't know what will."

He gives me the ghost of a smile and opens his mouth—then freezes.

A ten-foot fence rises before us, topped with wicked looking barbed wire and festooned in signs as brightly colored as candy wrappers. RADIATION HAZARD, they warn cheerfully. ARMY PERSONNEL ONLY. RESTRICTED AREA.

Beyond them lies the remnants of the agency base.

A thousand acres of char and ash spread toward the coastline. Half a dozen ships sit in an abandoned shipyard, hollowed-out hulls that'll never see their research missions. Directly below us is what used to be a parking lot, with chunks of uprooted pavement littered throughout. In the desert of black and gray, a few structures still stand: a singed warehouse here, a skeletal dormitory there. But almost everything is flattened and scorched.

The memorial was a sea of empty caskets.

"Why—" Quint's voice is choked. He steps forward, winding transparent fingers through the fence links. "Why have you brought us here?"

I stand very still, because the panic of this place is welling up inside me like water through cracks in the earth. I form my reply with difficulty. "I didn't. You did."

He turns to deny it, a frown cutting across his face. Then he stops—realizing how I've been staying a few steps behind him while he was talking and distracted, letting him lead the way without thinking about where he was going.

He turns his back on me, staring out across the ocean of ash. "You think he's here. You think I led you to him."

I make myself reach out. My fingers hover an inch away from the fence. The panic increases, winding tight around me, choking off my breath. I hate this place. I *hate* this place, and of course it's where we'd all end up. "I think...I think all three of us are connected to the base, somehow."

He shakes his head, slow and deliberate. I'm not sure whether it's a denial or a plea.

"I'm sorry," I offer, only half my mind on our conversation as I try to beat down the panic. I can't allow it to prevent me from finding Matthew, if he really is on the base, but the anxiety is huge and threatening and I *hate* feeling this way yet again, hate the helplessness and the hopelessness and the sickening, all-consuming fear.

Quint inhales. "I'm fading, Cam."

I jerk back. My hand falls to my side as I turn to him, panic attack momentarily forgotten. "What?"

He's still staring out at the base, head leaned against the fence. He holds one hand out and the sunlight cuts through it like he's made of nothing but mist. "I noticed it after the train station," he says, his tone thin, "but I thought I was imagining it. This morning it was worse. I've been trying to get up the courage to say something since dawn."

I remember standing in front of Dr. Lila's computer, the green light making him look even more transparent than usual—and last night, the moonrise gleaming through his torso. I thought I'd been imagining it too.

He closes his eyes. "If I could sleep, I think I'd have nightmares about this. I just keep fading and not knowing why until one day you get your wish and I'm gone completely. And then what happens to me?"

His words echo in my mind: *I'm afraid of the dark.*

This is his last-ditch effort to make me turn around. He's laying all his cards on the table—and it doesn't matter. I can't change my mind, not now that I know Matthew has something to do with the base explosion, something to do with Mom.

And something to do with time travel.

The desperate hope is back, the same kind that made me go with Matthew in the first place when he told me my brother wasn't exactly dead. Because if time travel is possible, if there are more alternate realities, if there's even the tiniest chance that some version of my mother isn't exactly dead either...then I can't turn back. Not until I know. Because the thing is, I don't think I care anymore what it means that she was shaking hands with Matthew. I don't care if Kyle was right to doubt her, and I don't care if she was conspiring with rogue agents. Even if the very worst of it is all true, even if I never really knew her at all—I still just want her back. And if there's any chance Matthew can work that miracle, I'll do anything he wants.

Quint turns, sees my expression. Neither of us has to say anything. He gives a nod, half bitter and half resigned, and steps through the fence.

He waits, exactly ten feet and three inches ahead of me, his back turned as I get up my courage. The panic ebbs and flows, peaking when I find a slit in the fence a few yards away—and then it glues my feet to the ground, weighs me down and locks me up, digs its claws deep and doesn't let go. I can't move. The fence and the fear both loom in front of me, insurmountable, impossible. If I set foot through that barrier, the panic will spiral out of control and it'll never stop.

But I've failed my mother once in this place already. She's dead because I couldn't face my fear. I can't, I *won't* fail her again.

So how do I stop the panic? Maybe she was right and the only way to fight it is to stop trying to fight it. I thought I didn't know how to accept something that felt so awful but now I think maybe this is how. Stepping through the fence, even if it kills me.

So I do.

And we search. For hours we search: fields of barrels filled with potentially radioactive ash, sealed and left behind until the Army can dispose of them properly. Vast, gutted warehouses that echo with my footsteps. I even venture out onto the decks of a few of the ships, but they're eerie and lifeless and I quickly return to land. The same smell lingers no matter where we go—burnt steel, charred plastic, something toxic and inescapable. It feels right.

The anxiety rages through me like a forest fire the whole time, and I do my level best to accept the hell out of it. I think maybe Mom would've been proud. The thought keeps me going.

The sun is low in the sky when we stop. I'm running on two hours of sleep and no food, and no matter how much I need answers, I can only push myself so far. I find a warehouse at the edge of the shipyard and settle down in a corner, desperate for rest, for an escape from the still-crushing fear. Sleep comes slow and blurred, a subtle, unsettled shift into unconsciousness.

Despite my best efforts, I dream.

CHAPTER FIFTEEN

THREE WEEKS AGO

COOL MARBLE UNDER MY FINGERS. The earth shaking beneath my feet. A handsome stranger in a lab coat, knocked to his hands and knees by the unexpected earthquake.

He staggers and lifts his head, peering around himself like he's not sure how he got there—and then his head jerks like he's been slapped and he stares to the north. "No," he breathes. "Oh, no."

I reach out to steady him. The ground throws him off balance again and his fingers grip mine, strong and solid, but he's not looking at me and the expression on his face is as terrified as my own probably was just a few seconds ago. At least he has a good excuse, not some crap anxiety disorder he should've beaten months ago.

"It's okay," I offer, nearly shouting to be heard above the rumbling. The ground quivers one last time and then goes still and I lower my voice to a normal volume. "Just an earthquake. Though it's rare for them to hit this part of the coast." I tighten my grip on his hand a little, trying to anchor him the way I'd want to be anchored.

His gaze jerks to me then, bright green and frantic. He yanks his hand away and pats his pockets like he's searching for something. He spots a pen and a cracked phone on the ground and sweeps them up, then stabs at the power button on the phone.

"Sorry, you're SOL there," I say, gesturing at it. "The towers are down or something. Everyone's been complaining, no one can get a signal."

He curses, still scanning the ground around his feet. "Paper," he snaps. "I had a piece of paper too, and a—a rock."

"A rock?" I ask, but he doesn't answer, so I shrug and bend down to search beneath the fountain's rim. A piece of paper is fluttering in the shadows, pinned beneath a strange shimmering chunk of what looks like metal. I scoop up both. The paper is scribbled with a string of illegible numbers and the rock is strangely soft and pliable, like I might be able to dent it if I squeezed hard enough. Some sort of gold alloy maybe? It's the wrong color though: a crisp quicksilver gray, like a lake in the wintertime.

I turn back to the boy and offer him the paper first. Relief washes over his expression as he reaches out, lifting his pen like he's about to write something else on it. Our fingers touch—

All the birds on the base scream, throwing themselves from trees and buildings and statues. They swirl into the air, climbing, clawing for the sky. Feathers float down from the chaos; one lands on the fountain, balancing delicately on its edge before it teeters into the water.

Together, we stare up at the birds. A shiver traces across my skin.

"Why..." I start, and then the world explodes.

CHAPTER
SIXTEEN

WHEN I WAKE UP, THE nooks and crannies of the warehouse are heavy with the smell of coffee.

Quint is leaned against the wall keeping watch. He stirs, looks down. His gaze is flat and tired as he scans my expression. "You remembered more," he guesses.

I sit up, run a hand through my matted hair. The anxiety is still present but it's died down a bit—more like a hot coal than a forest fire now. "Yeah," I say blearily. "About you. Us. The day we met, when you were alive."

"I don't want to know." The words drop through the dark like stones in a pond.

"Okay." I stand up.

"You still sure you want to find him? Sure you want to

know what he knows?" he asks, pushing off the wall and turning toward the exit at my side. The shadows wrap him up and blot him out, but only in the way they do for everyone. In the dark, all anyone has is a voice.

I take a breath: ash and coffee. Half toxic, half tempting. "I have to."

We step into the starlight.

The ruined base is quiet and calm, the cold moon shining dully overhead. On the distant horizon lightning flickers over the ocean and heralds yet another unseasonable storm. We wander, following the out-of-place smell of coffee, and end up at the shipyard. A newly lowered plank leads to the deck of a defunct research vessel, one of the ships I didn't get to explore earlier. In its past life, the boat must've been green and white, but now it's covered in scorch marks and bird droppings. Three-foot-tall letters splash white against the bow: *The McKay.*

I hesitate, squinting at the deck. I test my weight on the plank and then step out. Twenty feet below, algae-clogged water waits.

Half a dozen pigeons are perched on the ship's rail, heads tucked down in their feathers, murmuring sleepily to themselves. A few yards away from them sits a steaming mug and an empty coffeepot.

I wrap my fingers around the chipped blue cup and pick

it up. Fissures run through its sides, fine cracks that would probably split wide open if I pressed hard enough.

The coffee smells amazing. I dump it over the rails.

Behind me, someone sighs. Matthew. "I thought you could use some, that's all. I didn't poison it if that's what you're worried about."

"That's right," I answer, my voice steely and my eyes still on the water. "You've already established your preferred murder methods."

He steps out onto the deck. I turn. He's traded his black hoodie for a button-down gray shirt, and the effect makes him look almost normal—hands in his pockets, exasperated look on his face, glasses endearingly crooked. But the handle of his gun is poking out of one pocket, and I can still remember him giving me that same exasperated look while he was ignoring the janitor who was dying right behind him.

We watch each other. The leftover heat from the cup seeps into my hands.

"Aren't you worried about the radiation?" I ask, nodding at the fence lined with warning signs.

His mouth quirks humorlessly. "Aren't you?"

"I have bigger problems," I say, my tone flat. It's true in more ways than one. It's only because I've been so preoccupied with my anxiety, which exists only inside my own head, that I haven't had time to think about potential radiation poisoning, which is what I *should* be scared of. But in any case, I'm pretty sure I'd have to stay out here much longer than a single night to get a lethal dose.

Matthew nods. "Same here." Then, after a moment: "Sorry I couldn't let you know where I was sooner. The north end of the base is still manned by a handful of agents. Couldn't risk revealing myself."

"Maybe *I* should reveal you," I murmur. "My brother tells me you're a terrorist. Even your own ghost is afraid of you."

Quint looks away.

Matthew lifts one shoulder in a shrug, but his eyes are sharp and careful. "You could turn me in. But I don't think that's why you're here."

"So tell me why I'm here," I challenge.

"You're here because you have no one else to turn to," he says. No hesitation, no uncertainty. "You're here because I have the answers you've been searching for. But mainly, you're here because you've figured out I know your mother, and because you think I can bring her back."

Silence. Stillness. The pigeons rustle and settle.

He waits. Gives me one last chance to run, now that he knows I can't.

The mug creaks and grinds under my grip. "Tell me everything," I order.

And he does.

———

Six months ago, Dr. Matthew Lerato was a pacifist.

When he was first recruited by the agency, they placed him on teams that were creating weapons, new types of exploitable energy, anything that would give the military an edge or keep them funded. He requested reassignment. They resisted. So Matthew compromised with nonlethal weaponry, clean energy resources, and groundbreaking physics research.

But he had a pet project.

Leratonium, he called it. A brand new lab-created element that, combined with the right type of radiation and an electricity based trigger, could remove and store souls. The consciousness of a human being, transferred to inanimate storage until science could find a way to build it a new body. He couldn't prove it worked, of course. Not until they did human trials, which wouldn't take place until after years of research and testing.

The agency disagreed.

Where he saw the Holy Grail, they saw a power source. He'd developed a way to analyze the unique energy signature of a human consciousness, and it was vast—more than the yearly power output of the whole of North America. The agency took his research to Washington, and they quietly approved it for human trials.

Dual usage, they said: a weapon plus a near-endless

energy source. Plug in the consciousness of your enemies and use it to power your country.

Matthew was horrified. He went to his department heads, but they did nothing. So he went to the psychiatric division, the team that was partnered with his to study the psychological repercussions of consciousness storage. He chose Dr. Marianne Kingfisher and told her everything. She agreed the experiment had to be stopped and started working overtime, quietly gathering evidence that could be used to obtain a court order against the agency. But her methods took too long, and a week before the first Leratonium trial was scheduled, Matthew decided to sabotage it himself. A few recalibrations was all it took to ensure his research would self-destruct with no collateral damage.

But his bosses suspected he was getting cold feet, so they'd told him the wrong date. And five minutes before the real trial took place, Matthew realized that in his rush he'd gotten the calibrations for the electric trigger wrong. With the present settings the experiment was likely to destroy half the base and spread radiation over the coast. He started writing down the new calibrations and headed back to the base to correct them.

He was too late.

There was also a girl.

In her timeline, she was holding the brand new element when the experiment started leaking radiation into the base.

Leratonium was a stable element.

Under normal circumstances.

———

I squeeze the mug. My knuckles are white, and my breath is coming too fast.

"The radiation changed the Leratonium's properties, fused it to your cells," Matthew concludes. His hands are still in his pockets like this is nothing more than a casual conversation for him. "Kind of like lead poisoning. Though I'd need to take a sample to be sure."

The darkness is thunder in my ears. A kaleidoscope tumbles through my mind: holding Matthew's hand while the world exploded. Waking up with his consciousness tied to mine. My veins, glowing ghostly white with a metallic signature.

My mother, gathering evidence to stop the experiment. To save people's lives, not take them.

Her empty casket. Telling the ghost on her voicemail that I loved her.

I'd been lying to myself when I said I didn't care anymore whether she was guilty. Because I do care, I care *so much*...but with the knowledge of her innocence comes the certainty of my guilt.

It *is* my fault. She died because of me.

There's something I need to ask. Time travel. I need to ask about time travel, about alternate realities, about saving Mom. The words are there but I can't get them out, can't stop thinking about what I've done—

And what he's done.

Half my family. Matthew Lerato has killed half my family.

He's still talking. "The agency has been searching for me ever since the explosion. Not because I'm responsible for thousands of deaths, but because they want to force me to rebuild my destroyed research. They're about to get shut down by the investigations unless they can prove they're valuable enough to keep around, and Leratonium is their 'Get Out of Jail Free' card. In your timeline, they were using you for the same purpose—planning to reverse engineer the element based on your medical data, planning to get you to cooperate no matter what it took. Once I started to suspect that, I kept an eye on you until you stole that tablet and I could use it to verify my suspicions, and then I set the bomb to kill you and stop them—but that was before I knew what you could do, before I knew how much more versatile the element is when it's bonded to human cells." His voice is low, his eyes bright with fascination. "You're a new thing,

Camryn. You drew out my—Quint's—consciousness just by touching him. You can instinctively wield it as energy in life-or-death situations. To shift between timelines. To heal yourself. To survive an un-survivable explosion. I bet he's probably fading, right? Every time you use him up?" He's leaning forward now, too interested in his own damn science to even acknowledge what he's done.

"Go away." My voice is hoarse.

He frowns and pulls back, switching gears too late. "I'm asking for a reason. The timelines—"

But it's too much. I drop the mug. It hits the deck with a dull *thunk* and breaks clean in half, showing its white ceramic insides wormed through with cracks. "Go AWAY!" I shout, and the words roar in my ears and bounce into the night and send the pigeons flying. They jostle and shove, a jumble of flapping wings. A feather spins down to balance on the rail a few feet away.

I close my eyes.

Matthew exhales. He retreats. Footsteps, a muttered curse, the deck creaking in the night.

Quint is sitting next to me. I can feel him there even with my eyes closed: miserable, hollowed out. "This is what you didn't want to remember," I say. The mistakes he's made. The monstrous weapon he gave the agency, and the lives it cost to stop them.

He breathes. "I think so," he answers at last, and his despair vibrates between us like a plucked string.

I open my eyes. In the faint starlight, the charred earth of the base is pocked and shadowed, an alien planet. The feather is still balanced on the railing. A breeze whispers across the ship and ruffles it, but it settles back in the same spot. I reach for it, intending to knock it over the side and out of sight.

"I'm not him," Quint says, but the words are flat and desolate like he can't quite manage to believe them.

The feather tickles my palm. I curl my fingers tighter and it crinkles in my grip. All this time I've wanted the truth about the explosion that destroyed my life. And all this time it's been standing right next to me.

But still—

I'm not sure I'd like myself.

Don't make me remember.

All I have is you.

"Right now, all I have is you too," I tell him at last. "And I need you to be Quint."

"I'm sorry," he says to the stars, because he can't be Quint. Not really. Not anymore. Not after this.

I let go of the crumpled feather. It drifts down to the algae-coated water and, slowly but inevitably, sinks.

"So am I," I say.

I bring the coffee pot with me when I go to find Matthew. He hasn't gone very far. He's standing on the opposite side of the deck, hands in his pockets, peering out at the ocean. It's frothy and restless tonight, churning itself into a bruised green and brown beneath the storm clouds that flicker in the distance. Beyond the tiny beach outside the shipyard, toward the northern end of the base, two distant yellow figures bob between piles of rubble—agents in hazmat suits, checking for intruders. They probably heard me yell earlier. I could yell again right now, let them know exactly where we are. It should make me feel safer. It doesn't.

I stop a few feet away from Matthew. Just over his left shoulder, a hundred yards inland, is the outline of a demolished building. In the corner, where my mother's office used to be, a single jagged pillar is still standing.

My nails dig into the coffee pot's handle. It's so unfair. So *unnecessary.* There were so many ways she might have lived: if I'd picked her up on time, if Matthew had recalibrated sooner or more carefully, if the agency had waited until the day they were supposed to do the trial. But everything went exactly wrong and now she's gone. She's *gone.* I make myself think the word, make it hard and clear in my mind, because it's true. Whatever happens next, there's very little chance that will change. I should leave now, go home to Dad, let myself grieve and work through my guilt like a normal person. I shouldn't be talking to her murderer on the slim chance that whatever he hasn't told me yet has something to do with the possibility of bringing her back.

But still—time travel. Alternate realities. Not exactly dead.

I square my shoulders, step to Matthew's side, and set the empty coffeepot on the railing next to him with a *clank*.

"The storms are getting worse," he says mildly, still looking at the ocean.

"You led me here on purpose," I say without preamble, jerking my head at the coffee pot. "Tell me why."

He sighs and runs a hand through his hair, which flops right back down over his glasses. The lines in his face are deep and tired and make him look ten years older. "I should have led with this, but I'm sorry for what I've cost you, Camryn. Everything I've done, everything I wanted to base my whole career on, it's all to *save* lives. That's still all I'm trying to—"

"Don't," I cut him off. "Just tell me the rest of it."

He looks back out over the ocean and, after a moment, obeys. "When the base exploded I was just outside the blast range, still writing down the calibrations. Afterward, I was…" He taps his fingers against the railing. "Devastated."

In the distance, the ocean churns.

"And desperate to find a way to fix things," he goes on. "One of my team's other projects involved time travel, through wormholes mostly. We were closer than anyone had ever gotten. But it takes an astronomical amount of power to keep one open for even a millisecond, so we ended up scrapping the project without ever getting past the theoretical stage. After the explosion, though, I was uniquely motivated." He gives me a wry smile. "I stole from power facilities across the whole coast."

My gut tightens. "So it *is* you who's been screwing with the universe."

"It's not as easy as it sounds. Normally, there's no way of securing a wormhole on the other side—in the past, or the future, wherever. So even if I *could* power it, there was no way to control when I'd end up. But then I found out that the radiation released at the moment the experiment started, it created a sort of marker in space-time. An anchor for the wormhole." He motions at the base. "Traces of that radiation still linger here. I discovered that if I opened the wormhole from the base, I could set it to go back to the exact moment the experiment started. It was my chance to fix things. Fix *everything*."

His words burn fierce and bright with a dangerous sort of desperation, and my hand tightens around the coffeepot handle in response—because I know that burn, I know that despair. *Fix everything.* It's all I could ever want. But...

"You can't," I say, because here we are.

The light in his eyes goes dim. "No," he says, "I can't.

The power requirements are enormous. And the more I steal, the greater the chances the agency will track me down before I can open the next wormhole. I've tried again and again with as much power as I can scrape together, but it's not enough. It's never enough. I go back, inhabit the past version of myself for one second, two seconds. Enough time to create a few miniscule changes in hopes that they'll cause a ripple effect that will end in the explosion never having happened. Instead, it happens over and over again. Over and over again, I end up back here." His hands grip the railing.

"The grandfather paradox," I say numbly.

He sighs and nods. "Every time I go back and change something, it creates a new alternate timeline. I developed a way to travel between them, though it costs me more energy than I can spare, and that's how I found out about you." He pushes off the railing and looks at me, and just like that the conversation shifts, turns and tightens like a funnel cloud touching down—because he's coming to the endgame now, coming to whatever his reasons are for telling me all of this, and his eyes are burning again in a way that tells me I'm not going to like them.

I take a step back.

His gaze follows me, but he doesn't move. He doesn't have to. He's got the gun, and he's got the information, and I'm a hostage to them both. "Yours was the last timeline

I created," he says. "Before a few days ago, your version of Camryn Kingfisher didn't exist. You were dead in the explosion, every time. Your survival was an unintended ripple effect and it only happened once."

My stomach roils. I shake my head.

He cuts me off before I can protest. "Oh, your timeline is real. Your experiences are real. Everything you've been through in the last three weeks is exactly as valid as the original version of reality. That's the problem." He motions at the horizon, at the storm off the coast. "Each new timeline I create competes with the rest. The space-time continuum wasn't meant to branch off like that, wasn't meant to bear so many different versions of reality. Soon it'll start causing bigger side effects than just the storms. There will be atmospheric anomalies that suffocate cities, gravitational instabilities that swallow the stars. Eventually it'll be catastrophic."

He says it simply, like he's said it a thousand times before. Side effects. Instabilities.

Catastrophic.

And here it is: the endgame. I can see its corners and edges, its purpose and its potential, but the biggest part is still hidden. He's used energy he can't afford to track me down, put himself at risk to give me all this information, and that can only mean he wants something from me.

"Tell me," I demand, and I hate that my voice shakes.

The corner of his mouth twitches up in that familiar, humorless half smile. "I already told you. I need your help."

"For what?"

"For him. Quint."

A terrible suspicion tugs at my mind, a riptide in the dark. I take another step back.

This time, Matthew follows. "For the version of me that's dead, that's tied to your cells, that despite being partially used up to heal you and shift timelines still has enough energy left to power a continent for months."

At my side, Quint turns his back. He knows. How far did we get into this conversation before he guessed its outcome? How long has he been trying to figure out a way to keep me from this moment, this choice?

I bump into the railing. It digs into my spine. Nowhere else to go, except overboard.

Matthew stops. "Or," he says, "a wormhole, for just enough time to fix the biggest disaster in both our lives."

CHAPTER SEVENTEEN

MY THOUGHTS ICE OVER, CRYSTALLIZE. My mind glitters cold and bright with all the things I shouldn't be thinking.

Cherry rhubarb sauce, bright like blood against shattered glass.

A fountain. A boy huddled at its edge, knees drawn up and back turned.

...one day you get your wish and I'm gone completely. And what happens to me then?

I'm afraid of the dark.

"You want to use him up," I say. "You need *me* to use him up." Because otherwise, Matthew wouldn't be asking. He'd have taken Quint's energy by force and left me where

I fell, one more casualty of his greater mission.

I meet Matthew's eyes. He sees the ice in mine.

He tries again. "He's already dead anyway. If I succeed, you won't even remember him. And if I fail…" he motions at the storms off the coast. "Then it'll all be over soon enough. Please, help me fix this. I can save your mom. I can save *everyone*." He holds out his hand—an invitation. An offer.

And all at once I can see it, this thing he's offering me. It leaks through the ice, seeps into my mind like a spreading inkblot: the undamaged base rising all around, crowded with scientists and soldiers and researchers. My mother in her office. My brother at our home. My world would be therapy and homework instead of hallucinations and funerals and terrorists.

And all I'd have to do is kill Quint.

The vision vanishes and a crashing silence fills the space it left behind. I close my eyes and try to bring it back, but there's only one way to do that.

Panic claws its way up my throat. I turn to my ghost because he always knows what I should do, but he's staring at the sky with an empty gaze. "I'm still afraid," he admits, and his voice twists into something that's almost a laugh. "I thought if we got this far, if I found out everything, there would be nothing left to be afraid of."

And then he turns his head and meets my gaze and those

cut-glass eyes are deep and dark and bottomless. He's looking at me like he's expecting betrayal. Like he's expecting me to make the decision Matthew would make, the decision he's *already* made: one life for the greater good. One life for my family.

But another image flashes through my memory like a lit fuse—a trainmaster with empty eyes, his gaze locked on mine as he fades out of the world. *Not killing is an easy choice when you never have to make it*, Matthew told me afterward.

I've found out who my mother was. Now, I get to find out who I am.

I pick up the glass coffeepot and turn back to Matthew. "Find another way," I tell him and, before he can stop me, I smash it to the deck.

The sound shatters against the night. On the north end of the base, someone shouts. A flashlight beam sweeps toward us.

Matthew whirls on me. "There *is* no other way!" He curses, reaching for his gun as he peers at the agents.

I back toward the plank.

Matthew hesitates—and then his shoulders slump and something like regret sweeps across his features. He turns to me. "Fine," he says. For a second his tone is flat, resigned, and then he leans forward and the fire comes back, low and savage. "There's *one* other way, Camryn. Go to your timeline. Find my old equipment. And then come back, and tell me again that using Quint up is the wrong answer."

I inhale. He smells like mint and metal, cool and bitter and wintry. I take a long step back. And then another. And then, like I said I would never do again, I turn and run.

My feet pound on the plank and it shivers and creaks. I hit the blackened ground and the dirt feels crunchy, dry.

"Hey!" One of the agents who was searching nearby spots me. His hazmat suit glows a blinding yellow against the charred earth as his flashlight beam swings my way. A gate closes behind him and he breaks into a run, but I've got a hundred yard lead and tonight no one is going to catch me.

Past the warehouse. Around the fields of barrels. Through the fence, festooned with candy-bright warnings. The agent falls behind and gives up, shouting a few half-hearted threats before I'm beyond the range of his light and fleeing down the street, past the empty houses and the vacant offices, the shuttered windows and gaping darkness.

My legs are jelly. I can't go any farther. I stop in the middle of the abandoned road, gasping, clutching my stomach. And then, finally, in the shadows and the silence, I allow myself to think about what I've done.

Mom is gone. My version of Kyle is gone. The whole universe is fading out like a guttering candle. I could have paid a price and saved them all, but I didn't, and does that make me noble or a coward?

I press my hands to my eyes. The shaking starts low, somewhere in my gut.

Quint steps up beside me. All I can see are his feet. He's silent for a moment, and then he squats down at my side. I wrap my arms around myself and turn away and try to breathe. At the edges of my vision his lab coat rises and falls. He doesn't say anything, because what is there to say? Sorry, your mom is still dead, and now it's your fault even more than it was before?

I clamp my jaw. I will not break down in the middle of the abandoned street like a lost little girl. I choke in another breath and try to think, try to summon up some memory of Mom's coaching, try to remember some technique that might bring me back from the edge of the massive panic attack that's starting to sear the corners of my mind.

Grounding. I need to ground myself. Focus on the here and now, keep myself from spiraling. I look up, searching frantically for anything that I can use as an anchor.

Quint's left hand is on his knee. I focus on it, forcing myself to list as many of its characteristics as I can, trying to keep myself from getting lost in my own head—but all at once everything feels strange and unfamiliar and alien and *wrong*.

Derealization. This is just derealization, just another

symptom, just my brain flipping a switch and making everything feel weird and off. It'll go away after a minute, it always has. Focus. Concentrate.

Slender fingers.

Wide, square nails.

Slightly transparent skin.

Quint doesn't move, doesn't speak. I risk a glance upward. He's watching me. His expression is unreadable, but he nods like he's guessed what I'm doing and wants me to keep going. My concentration teeters—looking at him reminds me too much of the truth, of the impossible choice I've just made—and I yank my gaze back down to his hand. I wonder what it would be like to be able to hold it, to have someone real to anchor me. To have *him* be real.

I match my breathing to his. In. Out. Slow and deep.

Something is digging into my thigh through my pocket. It's the bracelet. The one Mom stole, the one I nearly got arrested over almost four years ago. And because I'm staring at Quint's hand I remember *her* hand: the way she added a flourish when she tossed the bracelet in the cup holder, the way she tugged at her ear when she grinned afterward.

I frown, the panic fading enough for me to think clearly. Her ear. The ear that should've held an expensive, brand-new pearl earring, her anniversary gift from Dad, but was somehow bare. I reach back further in my memory—but no, she'd definitely had them on when she'd come into the manager's office.

The answer comes with the moonlight, shifting subtly from behind a cloud, painting the street in silver. She'd taken the earrings off. She'd left them in the manager's office, in exchange for the bracelet I'd wanted so badly.

She hadn't stolen anything.

The world slowly rights itself. The vice around my chest loosens. I'm still shaking, but it's not as violent now, because at least I have this. It's too little, too late, but at least my mother was who I always thought she was.

Quint sits all the way down, legs stretched out at my side, and takes off his glasses. He doesn't clean them though, only folds in the earpieces one by one and then clasps his hands around them, uncharacteristically still. We both stare at the vacant house in front of us. Its windows have been broken, either from the explosion or from the looters who came through after. The remaining shards glitter in the starlight like a monster's teeth.

Quint breaks the silence first. "Do you trust me?" he asks. The question is an echo across a chasm; he's asked it once before, but time and knowledge have warped it into something wholly different.

I inhale a jagged breath. "No," I answer, because I shouldn't, not with everything I know now, but he hears the lie anyway and one corner of his mouth tilts up humorlessly.

"Good," he says. "Because I have a very bad idea, and I'd really like you to ignore it."

I swallow. "I'm actually pretty open to suggestions at this point."

"That's what I was afraid of," he says lightly, but one hand disappears from his lap—he's rubbing his face, probably.

My shaking slows a little more. Quint has a plan. A very bad plan, which he'll need me to enact for him. It's almost like old times.

"Shoot," I tell him, and my voice is even now.

"He said there was another way. His old equipment... in our timeline."

I lift my head but stop myself from looking at him at the last second. "Life-or-death," I remember.

His hand drops back to his lap and he blows out a breath. "Yes," he answers. "Life-or-death."

We both stare straight ahead. According to Matthew, my timeline switching abilities can be triggered by life-or-death scenarios. Failure would mean I wind up in a body bag, but success...success could mean finding another way to save everyone, a way where no one else has to die.

It also means using up a little bit more of Quint's soul.

I shouldn't say anything. I should let him offer this, let him do this, let *him* take the risks for once. Instead, I say:

"Why?"

I glance at him. He's still staring at his glasses, hair falling over his eyes. "For you," he says quietly.

Something breathless and a little bit fragile opens behind my chest. "Why?" I ask again, because I think I know what he means but I need to be sure.

His fingers curl around the frames so lightly. "Remember when I said I used to hate you?"

Mutely, I nod.

"I lied," he says, and climbs to his feet.

The breathless, fragile thing in my chest flips over, but I beat it back because I will *not* feel things like that about people who are dead and, one way or another, doomed. "And you're very good at it," I call after him instead, because I can hear the truths and untruths behind his words now as much as he can hear mine. And what he just said was the truth—but not all of it. He's still afraid, and he's still holding something back.

When I reach his side he's staring at the base. Beyond the warning signs, a flashlight beam is sweeping over the shipyard as the agent patrols for more intruders. The *McKay* gleams silent and unobtrusive in the starlight, nothing more than another empty ship.

Quint's mouth twists. "I used to be better, apparently," he says.

"Matthew? He didn't lie. He..."

"Manipulated," Quint finishes.

"Unsuccessfully," I emphasize.

He's still staring at the base. He sighs, closes his eyes. "Thank you. For running, when I know how much it must've cost you."

Suddenly I get the urge to step between him and the fence. I hate the way Quint looks right now—lost, scared, broken—and I hate Matthew for putting that look on his face. I want to protect him, which is ridiculous, because I can't even protect *me*. I curl my hands into fists and swallow the urge down, but I'm only partly successful. "Well," I answer finally, breathing past the lump in my throat. "It turns out I don't hate you either."

He opens his eyes. He glances at me. That lost look slips away, just a little, and something between us eases. That fragile feeling in my chest eases too. It should be terrifying, that connection—that vulnerability, that influence his feelings have on mine against all logic—but it's strangely comforting instead, and *that* frightens me even more. What will I do when this boy inevitably ends?

I shove the thought away, turn, and start walking toward the coastline. After a moment Quint follows, each of us keeping company with our own thoughts.

The sidewalk peters out, turns to a thin gravel path that

slopes upward toward the cliffs that guard the coast. We pass a few smokers and one or two midnight hikers, but it looks like this area was mostly abandoned after the blast.

"So what is this terrible plan you need me to carry out?" I ask at last.

"Switch timelines. Like I said."

"That's a goal, not a plan."

"You'll have to be the one to fill in the specifics."

"And here I thought *you* were supposed to be the genius."

He sends me a sideways glance. "We'll need a scenario that will make you panic as much as possible, because it sounds like overwhelming fear of imminent death and probably strong physical stressors are the key to kick-starting the shift. If we pick a situation that isn't big or deadly enough you could just wind up severely injured and have to use more of my energy to heal yourself, and then risk not having enough left over for a round-trip through timelines afterward. This has to be all or nothing. So you tell me: what type of death are you most afraid of?"

The question curdles in my stomach. I've been collecting a small mountain of new fears for months, and the prospect of facing down any one of them—even though I logically know they're all harmless—is petrifying enough. But he's not talking about triggering a panic attack, not talking about anxiety. He's talking about risking something well and truly deadly. And if I have so much trouble facing things that I know can't hurt me, how the hell am I supposed to be able to do something that really could kill me?

He slides his glasses back on. "I did tell you this was a bad idea. You sure you want to go through with it?"

"Yes," I say, and the word settles heavy in my bones.

I make a left turn. The gravel fades into a footpath, an old hiker's trail. It tilts up into a steeper grade. We climb.

"You should know," Quint comments when we're halfway to the top, "that even if the 'other way' works, it still might not fix everything."

I give him a look.

He shrugs. "This is exactly the type of scenario the grandfather paradox is supposed to explain. There's nothing to say that stopping the explosion won't simply create another alternate reality and make the universe implode faster."

"*Or,*" I reply, "it could snap the paradox loop shut because then Matthew wouldn't have had any reason to ever create any of the timelines in the first place, and everything will work out the way it should."

He gives me a look but doesn't reply. Instead, he says, "I'm assuming you've chosen your life-or-death scenario by now."

I keep my answer short because I'm already panting from the steep hike, and also because if I think about what

I'm about to do for too long there's a strong chance I'll change my mind. "I'm going to jump off a cliff," I tell him.

He arches an eyebrow. "You want to jump off a cliff in this timeline so you can continue falling to your death in your own timeline? Maybe we should make that plan B."

I hunch down and walk faster. "I'm going to jump over the ocean. Competitive cliff divers can jump from about sixty feet up and be fine, but that won't stop me from *feeling* like I'm about to die on the way down."

"Okay, but you're not a competitive cliff diver. Sixty feet is way too high for a beginner."

"I have to make it feel convincing, remember? Don't worry, I picked up some tips from Kyle." Not many, but it'll have to be enough.

"Right," Quint says. He doesn't quite sound convinced.

My fingernails dig into my palms. "There is one problem. I haven't quite figured out how to make sure we end up in the right timeline, since apparently Matthew has made more than one."

He mulls it over for a minute. "It sounds like using the energy is mostly automatic, instinctive—but maybe that's only a failsafe. Maybe you could figure out how to direct it consciously, with practice."

My lips flatten out. He talks about *the energy* and *practice* so easily, as if we weren't planning how to rip apart pieces of his soul. "We don't have time for practice," I say tightly.

He nods but says nothing. We keep walking.

The wind picks up the closer we get to the top, pushing me back, tugging at my still-matted hair. I hunker down and keep going—the best jumping-off points will probably be on the far side of the lookout, past the highest cliffs. Rocks skitter and roll beneath my shoes and I struggle to keep my footing. I crest the top of the trail, breathing hard—and jerk to a sudden stop.

I can see everything from up here. The sprawling city twinkles against the horizon, with the base a wide smear of gray right below. A broken down railing juts out over empty space a few yards to my left. To my right is a scraggly pine tree and a splintered picnic table…and a lone figure sitting on its bench, feet propped up on the seat of a dented motorcycle, hands behind his head like he doesn't have a care in the world and eyes so sharp I could cut myself.

We regard each other for a long moment. "Well, you look like crap," Kyle says at last.

CHAPTER
EIGHTEEN

WRAP MY ARMS AROUND myself. I want to hug him, and I want to punch him, and I want to run—but I can't do any of those things, because I have to save him, and that means I have to jump off a cliff.

"How did you find me?" I ask, stalling for time. I have to get him out of here. For the moment, this Kyle is the only Kyle I have left, and I can't make him watch me fall to my potential death.

His leather jacket rustles as he shifts in his seat, ignoring my question. "Dad hasn't been answering his phone today," he says instead, and the words are hard as granite. "And I'm glad. Because as soon as he does, I'm going to have to figure out how to tell him about you."

Not my dad, whispers my brain, but my heart lurches anyway. "How is he? Is he…okay?"

"He hasn't been okay for nearly a month now."

We watch each other. I glance at the cliff behind me and swallow. It's way too high, more than twice as tall as I wanted. If I'm forced to jump from here, I don't know if I'd survive, healing abilities or no. But do I have a choice?

"Kyle. I'm so sorry." The words slip out before I can stop them. He'll hear them as an apology for not telling him I survived the explosion, but what I really mean is: I'm sorry for killing you. I'm sorry I wasn't strong enough. I'm sorry I was too late.

It won't happen again.

Kyle drops his hands and leans forward, shadows dappling his form. He's wearing the same clothes as last night but now they're worn and wrinkled. His hair is even messier than usual, standing up in dark brown tufts, and he's got bags under his eyes like he hasn't slept in days. He sighs and rubs his face. "I have been fired," he says, and now the granite is gone and he just sounds exhausted. "I have been interrogated. I have been threatened with a court martial and a prison sentence, and my bosses only let me go because so far they haven't been able to find any proof that you—and by extension, me—are in fact aiding a terrorist. I suspect that'll change soon enough, though."

He pulls out a phone and tosses it to the table. A map glows on the screen, two tiny red dots blinking against the coastline. "Did you know my phone has a tracking feature?" he asks. "If it's ever stolen, this app can tell me exactly where it is even if the battery's dead. And a few hours ago—after I was released from the interrogation—I got an odd call from the phone company. Two signals, they said. Identical. They thought it was a data error."

My heart sinks and my hand goes to my pocket. To the phone that my Kyle gave me, the one I used to light our way in the tunnel, the one that saved my life. The one that's an exact duplicate of this Kyle's phone.

"But I thought it was suspicious, especially with everything else that's happened in the last twenty-four hours," he goes on, "so I followed the other signal. And do you know what I found?"

I stare down at the base, a wide swath of ash right below us. *I can see everything from up here,* I'd thought earlier. And so could he. The fields that I'd searched, the warehouse where I'd slept, the ship where I'd met—willingly, secretly, for the second time in as many days—with a known terrorist.

I squeeze my eyes shut. The edge of the cliff is three yards away. If I run, he won't be able to catch me. He won't be able to stop me, he won't be able to turn me in. "Please, just leave," I try one last time.

The bench creaks as Kyle stands. "How long have you known he was here, Cam? How long have you been working with him?"

"It's not what you think."

"Then tell me what to think," he says raggedly. "Tell me what I'm supposed to do now. Tell me how to get you out of this."

That look in his eyes, is that how I looked when I thought Mom was guilty? When I wanted her back anyway?

I take a long step backward. A blast of wind whistles up the side of the cliff, twisting at my shirt. "I have to get myself out," I tell him, and take another step. "I have to get us all out."

"Two more feet," Quint says quietly from somewhere to my left.

I open my eyes. If Kyle has to watch, so will I.

The cliff at my back is a steep drop-off, and it ends in a churning mass of waves and washed up debris from the base. This used to be one of my brother's favorite diving spots a few years back. There wasn't debris in the waves then, and as far as I remember from Dad's picnic at this spot last week, there isn't any in my timeline either—but if I'm wrong, or if I fail, or if the currents changed while I was gone, jumping in the ocean here will be as good as jumping in a blender.

It doesn't matter. Kyle won't leave here without me, and whether he turns me in to the agency or only to Dad, I won't get another shot at this.

"Mom hated you coming here," I tell Kyle, my eyes on the drop-off. "When you were seventeen, remember? You used to dive every weekend."

His gaze goes from me to the edge. "If you're thinking about taking it up yourself, you should probably pick a cliff that doesn't have chunks of buildings floating under it," he says slowly.

"But every time she lectured you about how dangerous it was, you only got more reckless. So one day she followed you." I take another step toward the edge. Six inches to go. "Middle of the night. Massive waves. The riptide was so strong, but you wouldn't stay home."

His eyes go tight and he takes a step forward. "Camryn," he says, in that too-casual voice that means he's starting to understand what I intend to do, "let's get out of here. We can reminisce later, okay?"

"She told me to stay in the car, but I snuck up after her, because I was so scared that you'd do something stupid. It turns out you weren't the one I should've been worried about."

He edges closer, one hand held out like I'm a wild animal he's trying not to spook, and now the wariness in his eyes is churning into full-blown fear. "Come here," he says, no longer trying to sound casual.

"She tried to stop you right before you dove, and you yelled at her. Said that she couldn't understand, that she wouldn't even try. She gave you a hug and said you were the one who didn't understand, because you'd never had to watch someone you love risk their life. Then she turned around, slid off her shoes, and took a running jump off the edge. It only took a few seconds for her to surface, but you didn't stop shaking for hours. That was the night you quit diving." I glance over my shoulder, into the roiling shadows a hundred feet below. "She's the one who taught me how far you go for family."

I breathe in. I meet Quint's eyes because I can't meet my brother's. And then I jump.

Kyle throws himself at me a second too late. He grabs for my arm, but gravity's already got a hold on me and I slip through his fingers, launching off the edge and over empty space. He shouts my name and reaches for me again and he sees the second he's about to overbalance—and he keeps reaching anyway.

Rocks crumble off the edge beneath him as he teeters. For half a second and an eternity, our gazes lock: this is how far he goes for family, too.

And then he's falling.

I scream something, but the words blur together and all I can hear is the way his voice cracked when he shouted my name and the sound his shoe made when it scraped against the edge of the cliff and the horrible screech of metal on charred metal far below. I stretch out my arm. The wind is howling and my stomach is pressing up against my ribcage and terror is pounding sheer and pure in my veins, but I will not let him hit that debris. I will not be the end of him. Not this time.

I feel the shift coming.

It's a river, a crashing torrent of instinct wrapped tight around my chest. It's a flood, a deluge, a tidal wave, and I curl myself around it as my fingers close on Kyle's shirt. Home. I am going home, and he is coming with me.

My knuckles brush his arm. An electric shock jumps between us.

I'm in the air, falling to my death—

And then I'm in the water, and my lungs are full of ocean, and I'm choking, drowning, spiraling in the dark. My spine feels cracked and my head goes bright with pain. Quint is gone. Kyle's fingers aren't in mine anymore and I don't know if it's because the ocean's current has ripped us apart or because he hit the churning debris a timeline away.

I flail for the surface, but I don't know which way is up and all my air is gone.

Calm people live. It's what Dad always says in his emergency management classes. So, against all instincts, I go limp—and then slowly start to float. Up is *that way.*

I thrash and struggle and break the surface. I choke out salt water and gasp in air. The current has already swept me a quarter mile down the shoreline, but there's no debris, no wreckage waiting to crash into me. This is a different time-line. I made it.

Did Kyle?

I want to call for my brother—but I've heard his silence once before, and I can't bear to hear it again.

But then: "CAMRYN!"

I jerk around. Past the tumbling waves and the jagged cliffside, an arm is waving against the stars. He's alive. I did it. Oh, God, I did it.

"Kyle!" I scream back. I try to swim toward him, but we're caught in crosscurrents and every second we spend in the water pulls us farther apart.

"Are you alright?" he shouts.

My arms are weak and my vision is blurry and my head is thundering with pain and adrenaline, but I don't care, because this time I've saved him. I've saved him, and—he's *here*. I can tell him everything, and this time he'll believe me. He'll help me.

I'm not on my own anymore.

"I'm okay!" I shout back, and for the first time in days, I start to allow myself to believe it.

"Good, because once you tell me what is happening I am going to *kill you!*" he calls back, but his voice shudders with relief.

A wave roars behind me, spinning me sideways and dunking me under. When I surface I can barely hear him anymore. He points up: at the cliff, the lookout point where we jumped from. We'll meet there. I try to signal that I understand, but another wave pushes me under and I give up.

I turn and paddle hard, parallel to shore like we were taught in water safety. Not too far ahead a tiny beach juts out from beneath the cliffs. I drag myself up and flop onto my back.

My wheezing subsides. My heart slows. The pain fades.

Waves wash ashore and pull away. The ocean breathes. After a count of fifty, I turn my head to find Quint has reappeared, lying at my side. He's staring up at the sky too, and there's something small and lost about his gaze. He's faded again. Not much, but enough that I can tell at a glance, in the middle of the night, that there's less of him than before.

His hand is between us. I lay mine atop it. Our fingertips brush, smoke on skin, and I don't feel a thing—but I *want* to. His touch should be warm, should be solid, should be electricity and vertigo and that feeling you get at the top of a theme park zip line right before you step out over the empty air. And what does it mean that I want that?

He turns his head and tries to smile. "We did it," he says.

We. We're a we again.

"Yeah," I answer, swallowing past the lump in my throat. "We did."

But he only looks away. The ocean washes in at our ankles and silence settles into the sand at our backs. As the minutes tick past, the waning sliver of a moon glows dimly overhead, barely there. Tomorrow it will be invisible.

"Do you think it's true, what Matthew said?" Quint asks at last. "That you won't even remember me?"

The ocean exhales, water foaming around my heels. I stare at the stars and picture it—my life, as it should be. I would never have been tied to Quint because he would never have existed. I want to think that some small part of me might remember him anyway, that when I saw someone cleaning their glasses I'd feel a twinge or that green eyes would make me think of him, but it's an empty hope. He'll be forgotten, completely. And is there any crueler end than that?

I keep my eyes on the moon. "I don't want it to be," I say, and I've never meant anything more in my life.

His chin dips and he sighs, then rolls to his feet. "We'd better get moving," he says, and starts toward the trail.

I turn my head and look at him: the boy who's letting me use up his soul piece by piece to keep it from being used up all at once. The boy who, even if our plan succeeds, will be erased from existence. The boy with no happy ending.

"Why'd you do it?" I call after him, unable to stop myself. "Why'd you let me jump if you knew it wouldn't change anything for you in the end?"

"I told you. I did it for you."

"We both know that's not the whole reason."

He stops, sighs again. "Because he was sweating," he says, his back to me.

I climb to my feet but don't start after him yet. "What?"

"Matthew. It's maybe seventy degrees tonight, and he was sweating." He looks at me over his shoulder, eyes weary. "He's scared too. He'll do anything to get what he wants, anything to fix the past, but not because it's the right thing to do. It's because he's afraid. He's so terrified of having to live with his mistakes that he's willing to screw with the entire universe to reverse them. If it was him in my place, him who couldn't remember anything, him who was being asked to give up his life to save the world—he'd have told you to keep running, and I know that because it's what I want to do too. And maybe I'm not brave enough to die like I should, but at least I'm brave enough to not be him."

He turns back around and starts up the trail. I watch him go, hardly able to breathe past the weight in my chest. I can't save Quint—so he's saving himself, the only way he can.

I follow him. The trail is steep, littered with beach grass and boulders and a brittle sort of quiet, the kind that shatters when it breaks. So instead of trying to tell him it'll all work out or that I'd give him a happy ending if I could, I try to focus on planning the next part of our mission.

The double of Kyle's phone is still in my pocket. If I show it to him and explain everything, surely he'll have to help me this time, especially once I can prove we're in a different timeline. Then he could get us into their system and figure out what and where Matthew's "old equipment" is. We'll steal it back, zip to the other timeline, hand it over, and fix everything.

My lips thin out. If I'm honest with myself, I don't like how Matthew told us about this other way: like it was a dare, a last resort. But the only other option is one I refuse to consider, and we can't turn back now anyway.

Thunder rumbles, low and ominous. Another unseasonable storm is on its way in and overhead the clouds are thickening. In the dim starlight that remains, I can barely make out the figure waiting at the top of the trail, staring out over the city. One hand clutches a phone, salt water dripping from his knuckles. The other is curled into a fist.

I hesitate. Deep breath. I try to step up to my brother's side, but he turns around before I can speak. "Go back to the beach," he orders, and if his voice was granite before, it's steel now, cold and flat and impenetrable.

My stomach sinks. Is he even going to give me a chance to explain? "I know you said you were going to kill me," I reply, struggling to sound breezy, "but if I get a vote as to the method, I've already had enough drowning to last a lifetime."

He doesn't move. "Go back," he says again, and this time the faintest hint of emotion colors the steel. It takes me a moment to identify it because it's a shade I hardly ever hear in Kyle's voice.

Fear.

I narrow my eyes and examine him more closely. His stance is wide, like he's trying to block the path. His phone is glowing and his hand covers most of the screen, but I can make out pieces of a message between his fingers: *APB* and *Camryn Kingfisher* and *potential act of terror.*

Quint has moved past us, cresting the top of the trail. He stops. "You need to see this," he calls, his tone laced with dread.

My breath stalls and I duck past my brother. Kyle grabs for me but misses. "Camryn," he says. The word reaches after me. Just that, only my name—but he says it like it's a warning, a prayer, like it's the only word he knows.

I dart to the top of the path and freeze.

My city is burning.

Sprawled beneath the cliffs, a wide swath of the suburbs is ablaze. The fire shifts with the growing wind, leaping from house to house at the edge of the destruction, and the smoke billows and coils and sifts through the gathering clouds. In the center of the smoldering rubble is a block that's almost entirely flattened—not from the fire itself, but from the explosion that started it. The train station.

That means we made it to the right timeline, then. But something else is wrong. Cold slivers of premonition prickle down my spine and I take a long step sideways, trying to shift my perspective, trying to spot the thing that's off. It takes me a moment to place it: not something I'm seeing, but something I'm hearing. Or rather, not hearing.

My city is silent.

There are no sirens howling to each other from the edges of the fire. No shouting refugees, no honking horns. To the west the stadium is lit up like the dawn, but there's no cheering, no booming commentary floating in snatches over traffic. To the far east is the Fort Wells airport, and its planes—white smudges from this distance—sit still and cold on their runways. I crane my neck but can't make out a single running light anywhere in the sky...except for a cluster of military helicopters that are circling off to the north like flies on a carcass, spotlights aimed down at the grid of streets. The faint buzz of their engines cuts clear across to my cliff even though there's no way I should be able to hear it above the clamor of my city. But that clamor, the buzzing heartbeat I've been listening to every day and night since Mom got stationed here three years ago—it's gone, and there's nothing left but the silence.

The slivers of premonition grow and spread like ice crystals in my veins.

My feet move. I stumble down the path, ignoring Kyle's shouts. The breeze is acrid and singed like burnt meat at a barbeque. I stifle a gag, pull my shirt over my mouth, and break into a run. The trees end. The buildings begin. The inhale and exhale of the ocean fades, and the silence grows until it's a living thing, a creature with claws and teeth and eyes that glimmer in the dark.

The first body is a hiker.

She's wearing a bright pink windbreaker and polka dotted sweatpants. The dirt around her is scuffed and there's grass under her fingernails. Lightning flickers, illuminating her face. Her eyes are open. She's staring at the clouds.

I check her pulse. Under my fingers, her wrist is cool and her body is rigid. She's been dead for hours, maybe a day.

I climb to my feet and run.

The second body is a security guard. The third is a teenager. The fourth is a homeless man, his little brown dog still tucked beneath his arm.

I stand in the middle of an intersection. All around me, cars are crashed into light posts, buildings, each other. The bodies inside are beginning to swell. I lean against a building, lungs burning, fingers splayed against the brick, and finally let myself understand:

My city isn't silent. My city is dead.

CHAPTER NINETEEN

NEEDLE-THIN RAINDROPS ON MY FACE. Cold fingers on my arms. *You have to tell me what happened,* my brother is shouting. *They think you did this.*

But all I can see are the cars, the bodies, the blood and the bloating, and all I can hear is the horrible thundering silence, and all I can think is:

Side effects. Instabilities. Catastrophic.

Kyle shoves his phone at me. **APB FOR CAMRYN KING-FISHER**, it reads, the screen dripping with rain and salt water. WANTED FOR QUESTIONING INVOLVING THEFT OF CLASSIFIED DATA AND POTENTIAL CITYWIDE ACT OF TERROR. SUSPECTED TO STILL BE IN THE CITY; ALL NEARBY AGENTS TO FORM SEARCH PARTIES. SEARCHERS' AIRCRAFT WILL BE GIVEN AN EXEMPTION TO THE CURRENT NATIONWIDE NO-FLY ZONE.

And if Kyle was ever going to believe anything I said, if he was ever going to help me, he won't now. The agency knows I stole the tablet. They know I lied to them. They think I had something to do with whatever killed the city, and Kyle is afraid they might be right.

But I know the truth.

This is what Matthew wanted me to see. This is why he sent me here. *Atmospheric anomalies that suffocate cities,* he'd said. And this is how he knew. There is no old equipment, no other way. There is only one alternative to murdering Quint, and this is it.

Time shrinks to a pinpoint, a blistering moment of certainty, and this is what I know: I will not allow that to be true. There has to be another way. I am going to make one.

The agents should have taken Kyle's gun. It's six inches from my face, snug in a shoulder holster, secured with nothing but a button. My brother's hands are on my shoulders, and his eyes are on mine. He follows my gaze too late.

I unsnap the button. I draw the gun. I take a long step backward, point it at the street, flick off the safety and fire.

Crack. Crack. Crack. Three bullets. Three holes in the asphalt. Three signals to tell the search parties exactly where I am.

Kyle moves to stop me. I lift the gun and aim at his torso. My finger isn't on the trigger now, because there is no force on earth that could make me put my finger on the trigger, but all he sees is the barrel of his gun and his sister's face behind it. He slowly lifts his hands and raises his eyes to mine, betrayal etched impossibly deep into the lines of his expression. "Camryn," he says again.

Like a warning. Like a prayer. Like it's the only word he knows.

Shouting echoes in the distance. Agents, coming to catch me.

"I have to get Matthew's equipment," I tell Kyle, and my voice cracks but the gun stays steady. "I have to turn myself in, and you have to run."

Kyle will be safe and I will face the agency. I will tell them I know what destroyed the city, and I will make them give me Matthew's old equipment—which *does* exist, it has to—in exchange for that information, and this will work because it's the only option I will allow to be true. No one else will die because of me. Not my family. And not Quint.

Kyle's gaze goes from me to the gun, which is still pointed at him. He lowers his hands and something shifts in his eyes.

He steps forward. He takes the gun from me gently, like it's fragile, like it's a thing crumbling bit by bit that he has to hold together. His fingers brush across the barrel, wrap around the grip. He lets out a breath, lifts the gun, and aims it at me. "No," he says. "I don't."

The granite is gone. The steel is gone. It's just me and my brother, and a ghost, and a gun.

And because I have nothing left to lose and nothing else to say, I let my hands fall to my sides and I raise my eyes to his and I ask the thing I've wanted to ask of him ever since he abandoned my bedside to return to his agency job the morning after our mother died.

"Kyle. Choose me," I tell him, and my voice breaks, but I don't care. "Not the agency. Stay with me. Believe *me*." The plea is nearly drowned out by the storm, but he hears it anyway.

Rain streams over the gun. No one moves. No one speaks. His expression doesn't change.

Thunder clatters. Someone shouts from a block away. Lightning illuminates the scene in brilliant strobe-light blasts: two agents running toward us, yellow hazmat suits burning like torches against the dark. They aim their guns at us both. They shout to Kyle and he shouts back, neither of us looking away from each other. The agents' guns shift to me. Kyle holsters his weapon. Steps away. He turns his back as the agents push me against the brick wall, snap cold metal handcuffs tight around my wrists, say something about my rights and acts of terrorism that void them—but I'm too numb to hear the words. I'm too numb to do anything but stare at my brother as the bricks scratch lines in my cheek and think about how he's failed me, and how I've failed him, and how our whole world is balanced on my choices and I've made the wrong one.

The sharp rain turns to hard-flung hail, bouncing pellets that spray against the street and threaten to rip holes in the agents' suits. They shout about shelter, about reinforcements being delayed, about safety. "Three blocks south," Kyle suggests.

Three blocks south. My brother is taking me home.

⸻

I'm sitting on our couch, but all the cushions are gone. An agent is slicing them open one by one, dragging her hands through their innards, pulling out fistfuls of feathers that drift to the carpet. She's already ransacked the cupboards, the beds, the closets. She won't tell me what she's looking for, but the government already has all the evidence it needs to lock me up. Whether it's for one year or twenty, it'll be a death sentence for us all.

The other agent sits on the loveseat opposite me. His hazmat hood is in his lap, mahogany hands folded casually atop it like he's interviewing me for a job instead of asking me how I killed the city.

"Reinforcements will make it through the storm soon enough," he says. "It'll be easier if you talk to me first."

I look at Quint. He's sitting at my side, head bowed. He knows how this has to end. But my mind is still spinning like a top at the end of its life cycle, circling around and around the only option I will allow to be true. The equipment Matthew needs exists. I can still get it, can still save Quint. He deserves the chance to choose his own death, even if that's all I have left to give him.

I lick my lips. "I didn't kill the city, but I know what did. I'll give you the information in exchange for Dr. Matthew Lerato's old equipment."

Kyle is seated at the kitchen table. The window behind him is open and the storm beats against the screen like a wolf at the door. He's typing on his old computer, hacking into security systems and video surveillance from the train station, searching for evidence at the agents' request. I wait for him to see himself, to see that this world is different from the one we left, but his eyes never change and he never looks up.

"We don't negotiate with terrorists," says the agent without blinking, dragging my attention back to him. "Especially ones who set off dirty bombs in the hearts of major cities."

Riiip. The last cushion spills its feathers and slumps, gutless, to the ground.

Quint raises his head. He looks at me. Dirty bomb: an explosive device engineered to spread radioactive debris. So that's what Matthew did at the train station. It couldn't have been what killed the city—radiation sickness would take longer and have more obvious symptoms—but even if I got away from the blast, he must've wanted to make sure I wouldn't last for long.

A crooked smile stretches my lips. He didn't know he'd need me then. Joke's on him.

My mind wobbles, slower and slower. Kyle's fingers click against the keyboard.

"You must've had accomplices," the agent is saying now. "Give us some names, and maybe the judge won't try you as an adult."

The lights flicker. They're out for one second, two seconds, three seconds, then the room flashes back to bright. The bulb over the sink pops and goes out, rebelling against the power surge. My brother sits back, lips tight, hands in his lap as he waits for the Wi-Fi to reconnect.

The agent opposite me lifts his eyes to the ceiling. "Was it you who broke into the power plant, too?" he murmurs. "Did you think the surges would slow us down, that we wouldn't catch you?"

I'm twisting my wrists in my handcuffs now, back and forth, wearing thin red lines in my skin. They moved the cuffs to the front when we got here. I wonder if it should make me feel less helpless. "I didn't kill the city," I tell him again.

Kyle's fingers resume their tapping on the keyboard.

The female agent crosses the living room to start pulling down wall hangings and checking behind them, for hidden safes, probably. Mom's antique Celtic cross jangles against the floorboards, and Dad's Star Wars posters end up in a torn heap next to the door.

I look away. Dad would've been at work when it happened. I won't have to see his body. But somehow, the posters are almost as bad.

My mind teeters and sways. I jostle it into motion again. The equipment. I have to get the equipment.

The agents' walkie-talkies crackle. Reinforcements are twenty minutes out, unless the storm gives way sooner. My agent eyes me, letting the silence stretch, giving the deadline time to sink in. Then he turns and calls to Kyle. "Find anything yet?"

My brother stands up. His gun peeks out from beneath his jacket—it's still unsnapped. "Yeah," he says, eyes on the screen. "Warehouse 3 on the north end of the base. East quarter."

And then he raises his eyes. He looks at me. He smiles that old sharp-edged smile, like he's laughing at himself and laughing at the world and also not laughing at all, and a giddy sort of fear shoots down my spine. It feels like premonition. It feels like a burning city, too quiet in the night.

The agent frowns. He starts to ask a question, but I don't

hear him because my brother isn't looking at me anymore. He's looking at the agent, and he's reaching for his gun.

The gun is in his hand. It lifts up and snaps down. *Crunch.* The agent turns too slow. When the butt of the gun meets his skull he jerks forward and then slumps to the floor.

Kyle pivots. The female agent isn't fast enough either. He's already across the room, snatching her cuffs from her belt. A scuffle. The power flickers out again, plunging us into the dark.

One.

Two.

Three.

Crack! Muzzle flash singes the air.

The lights come back on. Another bulb pops. Kyle is next to the window, gun aimed at the agent. Her walkie is gone. One of her hands is cuffed to the table. The other holds her own gun, steady and outstretched, aimed at my brother. A standoff.

I'm on my feet, frozen, staring, breathless—and Kyle looks at me. It's only for a second, not long enough to give the agent an advantage, but in his eyes something shifts again and this time I recognize it. It's his decision.

He has no reason to trust me. He has no idea about timelines or Quint or the failing space-time continuum. All he knows is what he's seen: me, meeting with a terrorist.

Me, jumping off a cliff. Me, threatening him with his own gun. The agency calls me dangerous and he thinks they might be right, but it doesn't matter—because my brother has finally made his decision, and he's chosen me anyway.

Warehouse 3, east quarter. He wasn't hacking into video surveillance. He was searching the agency's databases. I told him I needed Matthew's equipment, so he found it for me.

"Kyle," I say, but can't get anything else out past the lump in my throat. Damn it, this is *not* the time to cry. We need to get to that warehouse. I can tell him everything after I save the world.

"Reinforcements are still eighteen minutes out," he tells me, "but you'd better take the fire escape to be safe. I'll hold them off as long as I can." Then he blinks a little, and with his free hand pats his jacket's breast pocket like he's looking for something. "Maybe not all that long," he amends, with a rueful note that wavers at the end. He drops his hand.

His palm is painted a slick, bright red, and the world stops turning.

———

Later, I will think: I should have stopped the bleeding. I will think: I should have been faster.

I will think: I shouldn't have picked up the gun.

———

His eyes don't fade like the trainmaster's. He closes them too soon. I'm kneeling above him, screaming his name, hands pressed uselessly to the wound—left of the sternum, right over his heart, blood spurting weakly between my fingers—while he dies. Again.

I don't know how long it took me to cross the floor and get to him. I don't remember when he fell, whether I caught him. All I know is that my palms are red like his, and that he's lifting his hand, he's touching my face. He's smiling. No sharp edges this time: all soft and dim and fuzzy, because he's in shock.

"Careful, kid," he says, eyes opening to slits. "You're in danger of looking affectionate."

The bleeding slows. His eyes close again, and stay shut.

———

Mom always believed in Heaven. Dad believed in the possibility of an afterlife with the skeptical sort of optimism most people reserve for buying lottery tickets. I believe in God, and in hope.

I don't know what Kyle believed. I never bothered to ask him.

In my peripheral vision, the agent is staring at me. Her hand twitches around her weapon. I wonder if she's killed anyone before. I wonder if she's felt this: a raging in her blood, a truth, a *wanting*. I can't feel anything, I can't see anything, I can't think anything except—

My brother is dead. It's my fault, again. But it's also hers.

I pick up the gun.

She doesn't hesitate because I'm a minor. She doesn't give me a warning. She tightens her finger around the trigger and fires, point blank.

Click. Nothing. The gun's jammed.

She curses. Yanks the magazine out.

I stand. I aim Kyle's gun. My brother is gone, my whole family is gone, and she could stop me from saving them. She could stop me from saving Quint, the only person I care about who's not already well and truly dead. Warehouse 3, east quarter: she knows where I'm going. When the reinforcements arrive, she can send them after me—and that's *if* she doesn't shoot me before I can escape, *if* she doesn't get out of her cuffs and find her walkie and tell the agency how to head me off.

She murdered my brother. I could make her pay.

Just in this timeline. Just for now. When I fix everything, it never would've happened. I won't even remember.

My blood burns, and the wanting blisters against it.

Not killing is an easy choice when you never have to make it. I glance at Quint. He's watching, hands at his sides, eyes dark and waiting. I wonder if Matthew's thoughts are running through his head too. I wonder if he's felt this kind of fury, if he's been this overwhelmed, if he's felt so absolutely helpless and then suddenly, breathtakingly, *not*. If Quint were holding the gun, would he justify this death the way I'm trying to? The way Matthew would?

No. Because he wants to be better.

A trainmaster with empty eyes. *That emptiness*, I'd told Quint afterward. *That's the thing I hate.* I hadn't understood how one person could do that to another. And now I do understand, and what am I going to do about that?

My hands are slick and sticky on Kyle's gun. The storm is beating against the window at my back. The agent is shoving the magazine back in, and I have one heartbeat to make my decision.

I ran from Matthew because I refused to be like him. I jumped off a cliff. I turned myself in. I let my brother follow, and I watched him die—all because I wouldn't be a murderer.

I choose the storm.

CHAPTER
TWENTY

TWO STEPS. I'M OUT THE window. The screen was already torn. My exit tears it wider.

Gunshot cracks behind me, a second too late. The agent misses. Splinters explode off the window's frame, shrapnel that slices into my cheek and my shoulder.

Thunder rattles the fire escape beneath my feet. Cuffed hands make the ladder impossible. I jump from the last landing instead, letting myself dangle first to soften the impact, but I still roll my ankle.

By the time I get to the end of the block, the pain in my foot starts to disappear. I try to make it stop, try to hang onto the white-hot ache, but it's like trying to make a waterfall flow backward. The ache fades. So does Quint. And I didn't kill the agent, but isn't this just as bad? Aren't I just as bad? I can't stop using him up, piece by piece. His soul for my failures. His life for my family's.

Another way. I'll find it if it's the last thing I do.

———

I run. In my mind, the top is still spinning, spinning, and I'm afraid of where it will land. Hail skitters beneath my steps. Rain drives down in sheets. The mental pictures are back, old mixed with new, flaring to life between flashes of lightning.

A tunnel in the dark.

Sixteen minutes before the reinforcements arrive.

A hiker with polka dotted sweatpants, grass beneath her nails.

Ten minutes. I can see the base.

Forty-weight oil and expensive aftershave. Torn posters heaped on the ground. Chestnut hair and a chewed-up pencil.

They're not dead, not really.

Careful, kid. You're in danger of looking affectionate.

The north end of the base is littered with dead agents. One of them lies in a gateway, preventing the lock from engaging. I squeeze through the gap, step over him without looking at his face. Warehouse 3. East quarter. Warehouse 3. East quarter.

Shelves. Crates stacked haphazardly, leaning into the aisle. A guard's body sprawled across a box. Labels gleaming dimly in the light of the dying flashlight I took from his belt. I have six minutes.

One crate is sandwiched in a tall stack. *Physics Department,* reads the label. And beneath that: *Dr. Matthew Lerato.*

I yank it out. The moment is clogged, slow, and it takes forever for the crate to fall.

It crashes. Papers fan out, spreading like a stain across the concrete. I stare for a long moment. Then I'm digging through the box, shoving aside tattered notebooks and loose pages—but there's no equipment. No machinery. Nothing but old research.

I turn back to the shelves. I search, scanning the labels. I had to have missed something.

"Cam," Quint says from behind me.

"No." I cut him off, because I know what he'll say, and if I don't listen it won't be true.

"Cam," he says again. "There is no equipment."

And in my mind, the top finally falls.

My cheeks are wet. I don't know when I started crying, and I don't know who I'm crying for. My father, dead in his hospital across town. The lost versions of Kyle, who I couldn't save. Quint, who I used to hate and then might've fallen for, and soon won't remember. Because if there is no equipment, then there is no other way. I've used Quint for nothing. Kyle died for nothing. And despite everything, this is how it will end: with everyone I love dead and me a murderer to bring them back.

I close my eyes. "Tell me to run."

"*Run*," Quint says, like the word is wrung out of him.

I think about the sliver of a moon. I think about the empty sky. "I'll find a way to save you," I tell him, but even I can't believe myself anymore.

The lights blink on. I turn around and open my eyes even though the brightness burns, because if this is the truth then the least I can do is see it. Useless papers at our feet, useless crates at our backs. The look on his face is devastation.

The lights go dark. I sink down and papers rustle beneath me. I kick them away and then, because it feels good to lash out, I kick them again. They scatter and crinkle underfoot.

One page drifts across the pile, face up. My mother's signature is at the bottom.

Gently, I lift it. It's a cover letter addressed to the court, referencing unethical use of scientific research. It's dated the day before the explosion.

If the agency had waited a few more days, a week, two weeks, she would've had enough time to gather all her evidence. She would've had time to stop them, or Matthew would've had time to recalibrate his sabotage properly. I wouldn't have to say goodbye to anyone else.

I set the paper back on the ground, softly. The edge is

traced in watery red fingerprints. I turn my hands over, cuffs tight around my wrists, palms rusted with my brother's blood.

"Do you believe in the afterlife?" I ask Quint.

He drops his hands in his pockets and gives me a twisted smile. "Considering you're about to kill me, I should get to pick the topic of our final conversation. And I think I'll choose something cheerier than what'll happen to me after said death."

My jaw clenches. "Quint," I say, and it's a struggle to get the word out because it's not what I want to say. What I want to say is *forgive me* and *don't leave me* and *I think I could have fallen for you,* but it's too little too late, because we've been on opposite sides of life and death ever since the day we met.

His smile goes flat. "I don't know."

I curl my fingers over my palms. "I want...I want to believe you'd go to Heaven. Or somewhere. God, anywhere." Not the dark. Not nothingness. Not forgotten.

He sighs and pokes at a paper with his toe. "Here's the thing," he says. "I don't think it's my soul you've been using up."

I stare at him. Something like hope flutters in my stomach, painful and precious.

"I don't think souls are divisible," he says. "You're not using up my consciousness a little bit at a time. I'm fading, but only my appearance. The real me, my thoughts, who I am, that hasn't faded at all. Which makes me think that consciousness and a person's energy are two different things."

I look down at the papers he's still nudging with his shoe. "You remembered more research," I say.

He shrugs. "I think it might've been your mom's theory, actually, after Matthew took his data to her." He nods at the bloodstained paper. "Looks like she spotted some measurements he took of end-of-life patients, how their energy spiked when they were dying and then suddenly dissipated. She hypothesized that the energy tethers our souls to our bodies—or to Leratonium, in my case—and then after we die, that sudden dissipation sling-shots our consciousness… elsewhere."

Mom's voice echoes in my head. *They dance like falling stars, twisting through the night, and then gather all their energy to launch themselves in a final brilliant flash into Heaven.*

My throat closes. "And what happens if all your energy is used up before it can send your consciousness away?"

He looks up and gives me a sardonic smile, but his eyes are shuttered. "I don't know. I drift, maybe, or sink. Or just…disappear."

The dark. The nothingness. The boy with no happy ending.

I remember him sitting on the fountain, knees drawn up and back turned. I remember cool quicksilver in my hand

and waking up with him tied to me. "I wish I'd never met you," I tell him.

He hears the lie and gives his own. "Me too." He slides down to the ground, feet splayed out, hands in his lap. "Do you think it'll hurt?"

My heart twists hard. I squeeze my eyes shut, trying and failing to make my voice come out level. "I thought you wanted to talk about something cheerier."

He ignores me and motions at the dead guard, visible in the other aisle from between the boxes. "Do you think it hurt for him? Was it fast? Will it be that way for me, since I don't have a body?"

My hands curl into fists. "*Stop.*"

His gaze snaps to me and his eyes go dark. "If you have to do this to me," he says, "it should be hard. You shouldn't get to only wonder about the afterlife because you want to imagine everything will still turn out okay somehow. You should have to *think*. You should have to *decide*. You should have to remember, too, but there's nothing we can do about that."

I jolt to my feet, hands still clenched. "You think it's easy for me? You think I *want* this? You think I want you to— to…" I can't even finish.

"Will it hurt?" he asks, implacable.

"I don't know!"

"You don't know if it hurt for the guard, or you don't

know if it'll be the same for me? Come on, you're medically trained. Give me your best guess."

I take a shuddering breath and stab a finger at the dead man. "It took about a minute for him to pass out. Not much longer for his brain to shut down. His heart gave in, and then his capillaries burst from oxygen deprivation. Are you happy now?"

"Are you?"

"Of course not, you jackass!"

"Why?"

"Because I can't lose you too!"

The words bounce between us. Quint's expression smooths out and he nods like I've just explained a complicated math problem he's been trying to figure out. I cover my mouth with a hand and think about taking both the words and impossible emotions behind them back, saying I didn't mean them, not like *that*, that he'd manipulated the conversation to make me say it—but I don't. Because even if that's what he wanted me to admit, it wouldn't have worked if it hadn't been true. If however I feel about him hadn't been true.

He waits to see if I'll take it back. When I don't, his eyes change, lighten. "Good," he says.

I suck in a breath. "How the *hell* is that good?"

"I don't want it to hurt," he says softly, "but at least I

won't be the only one in pain."

I swipe a hand across my face and exhale. "I was right before."

"About what?"

"You being a jackass."

He breathes out a laugh, and a little more of that terrible devastation eases from his expression.

I hesitate. "Are you—are you still afraid?"

"Oh, I'm terrified. Whatever it is we might be to each other, it doesn't cure that."

I stare at him. He gives me a shrug and an ironic half-smile, acknowledging what he's said and the terrible timing of it all—then, because he's not a total jackass, he waves a hand at the dead guard. "At least I don't have a brain that'll shut down, or a heart that will stop, or capillaries to burst. Maybe it won't hurt after all."

It's a truce, a gift. He's letting it be just a little bit easier for me, letting me think that maybe he'll be okay after all.

But I frown and go still. "What did you say?" I ask.

He raises an eyebrow. "Maybe it won't hurt?"

"No. Before that, the things you don't have."

He ticks the items off on his fingers. "Brain, heart, capillaries."

I turn around and peer at the dead guard between the boxes. Capillaries. Suffocation victims should have burst capillaries, especially in their eyes.

A flashback rises: *A hiker in polka dotted sweatpants, grass beneath her nails.* The lightning illuminated her face. Her eyes gleamed blue and white.

But not red. Not bloodshot.

My pulse quickens. I squeeze between boxes, leaving Quint where he sits, and kneel over the guard's body. He's bulky, Hispanic, late thirties. His eyes are dark brown. The whites gleam, polished in the glow of the stolen flashlight. No burst blood vessels for him, either.

I pick up a hand. His nailbeds are normal, not blue from cyanosis.

He didn't die from suffocation. None of them could have. This wasn't an atmospheric anomaly, not one of Matthew's side effects. Something else killed my city.

My hand tightens around the flashlight. I stand up and back away. Don't make assumptions, Mom would say. Observe the evidence. Form a hypothesis.

The agents—they'd been so sure I killed the city, so certain it had been an intentional act. And I hadn't even questioned why. What equation had they put together, whose sum I had missed? What was the evidence? There was the dirty bomb, Matthew's attempt to get rid of me before he knew he'd need me, though it still didn't quite make sense for him to spread radiation with it too.

And: *Was it you who broke into the power plant?* one of the agents had asked me. It had to have been Matthew who broke in, but why—to cut the power? To cause a surge? To trigger something?

Trigger. An electric trigger. Plus radiation.

My breath stalls. I know that formula. Oh God, I know that formula. But one piece of it is missing.

I'm moving toward the empty crate. I'm praying: please be wrong. Please, be wrong.

I pick it up, turn it around, hold the flashlight up so I can see the label. *Notebooks,* it says. *Research,* it says.

And at the very bottom, scratched in faint pencil:

Leratonium

The last piece of Matthew's old equipment. It was here, and now it's gone, because he's already used it.

I know what killed my city. I know *who* killed my city.

I drop the flashlight. It hits the concrete with a percussive crash. The fluorescents overhead blink on, flicker off. "Quint," I say, my voice distant and dreamlike, "what are the ingredients for a soul transfer?"

He's still sitting in the same spot. "Leratonium, radiation to activate it, and an electrical trigger to link the patient to the Leratonium," he says. "You were probably able to use your brain's natural electricity as the trigger when you drew out my consciousness, if that's why you're asking."

"That's not why I'm asking," I say.

He looks at me. Looks at the box. Reads the label and frowns—and then everything snaps into place for him too, and his eyes jerk to mine.

This is Matthew's other way. This is what he wanted me to see. This is the last piece of the equation, and its sum shines like too-bright silver.

He stole their souls. He stole the lives, the energy, of every single person in my city. And then he told me he'd been taking from *power facilities* to feed his wormholes, and I'd believed him.

I drop the box. I press my hands to my head. His logic burns through my mind like a lit fuse: everyone will be dead soon anyway, if he can't fix the space-time continuum. None of the lives he's taken will matter once he succeeds.

And why stop at one timeline? Why not use every resource at his disposal? He'd have done this again and again, every time he accidentally created a new alternate reality. Every time he failed, he'd kill another version of my city to power his next attempt at changing the past.

Except in his own timeline. Because there, he could be caught. There his mission could be jeopardized. But every other timeline, every other version of my family—gone.

The Kyle who just died was the only Kyle left.

"Did he tell you I was afraid?" asks a voice, and at first I think it's Quint.

I'm still holding my head. I don't look up. All I can see is the cement floor, blurry through my tears, and all I can hear is the tiredness and acceptance in that voice, and all I can smell is mint and metal.

I inhale. With the oxygen comes hatred. It sears my lungs, burns away the tears, grips my bones and holds them tight and *twists*.

I straighten. I drop my hands. When I speak, my voice is even. "Funny," I tell Matthew. "I didn't take you for the lurker type."

He's standing at the end of the shelves, shadows pouring over him, watching me with those careful eyes. His steampunk gun sticks out of one pocket. Quicksilver metal coils around its barrel, and I finally recognize that shimmer for what it is. The janitor he shot, the trainmaster, their gazes were empty like something was missing. Because something was. Efficient in every murder, Matthew had taken their energy in addition to their lives.

He lifts one shoulder and nods at the dead guard. "You needed to see the other option for yourself. Because here's the thing," he says with a sigh, taking off his glasses and rubbing his eyes, "I *was* afraid. I was afraid you wouldn't help me if you didn't understand, and now that you do I'm still afraid you'll let me fail. I'm afraid that my only contribution to the world will be to end it, and that I will run and run forever, back and forth through time, and the cost will get higher and higher and I'll never be able to fix any of it." His voice is raw by the time he's finished, and he sounds too much like my ghost and also nothing like him at all.

Quint is on his feet next to the empty crate. He's standing, staring, pale and frozen. He looks the same as he did the first time we met Matthew: ghostly and empty, barely a memory. Nothing more than an afterimage.

And then he looks at me. Something comes into his eyes that looks like life, and he draws a breath. He steps forward. He stands in front of me to face his double, so that I have to look through him to see Matthew. And the twisting hatred doesn't ease, but a sense of safety settles in alongside it. I remember what I thought when Kyle jumped off the cliff after me, when I found him safe in the ocean—that I wasn't alone anymore. But the truth is I've never been alone. Not since I found a boy next to a fountain and accidentally hid his soul in mine.

I look through Quint and speak to Matthew. "He did tell me you were afraid," I say. "He's afraid, too. But that's not the important thing. I think there's only one difference between the best and worst versions of ourselves, and that's whether you choose to act on that fear, or be better than it."

Quint turns his head. He smiles at me, the type of smile

I've only seen from him a few times before—full, bright, lighting him up from the inside.

Somewhere close by, a door bangs and someone calls out. Agents. My time is up.

Matthew gives me an exasperated look and pulls something out of his pocket. He turns it over in his hand. "Maybe," he says. "Well, probably. But that better version of me still has energy that's a hundred times more potent than anything I can scrape together, even with all the souls I've taken, and I still need you to give it to me."

A shadow darts past the end of our aisle. Someone shouts my name and an order to surrender.

With his free hand, Matthew draws his gun and flicks a switch on the handle. It hums and buzzes just beyond the edge of hearing. Then he looks up and tosses me the other thing he was holding.

It careens through Quint. It arcs toward me. I catch it, my cuffs rattling.

It's a cell phone. Scuffed green case. Chewbacca sticker on the back. The wallpaper is a photo of my family.

Dad hasn't been answering his phone, Kyle said on the cliff.

There is only one reason Matthew would have this. One reason he would give it to me now. What better way to convince me to change the past, than to strip away all that's left of my present?

There was only one timeline where my dad was still alive. And now there are none.

The world goes silent. No blood roaring in my ears, no agents shouting at my back.

I look up. Fuzzy and indistinct on the other side of Quint, Matthew nods at me. He flips another switch on the side of his gun.

"See you at the ship," he tells me, and then disappears.

CHAPTER TWENTY-ONE

AGENTS EVERYWHERE. PAPERS BENEATH OUR feet, a carpet that rustles and slides. Quint is in front of me, back still turned, the moment hanging between us—a breathless, quavering thing.

The beginning of a shift coils around my ribcage. It tightens. It waits.

Quint turns his head. I can only see his profile, but his expression is clear and open. "Do it," he says.

I drop the phone.

───

The agent in front of me is blonde, short, with steely eyes and hands that don't shake. She's the one who killed Kyle.

Except she didn't. Because it was Matthew who stole the city's souls, Matthew who sent me here, Matthew's fault we got caught by the agents, Matthew who gave me an unthinkable choice—

But me who will have to make it.

I have to shift back to his timeline. I have to give him Quint. I have to save my family, even if I can't save myself.

The phone tumbles end over end, careening toward its own destruction.

The agent's gun is pointed at me. It won't jam this time. She's shouting at me to pull Kyle's gun out of my waistband—two fingers, no sudden moves, lay it on the ground and kick it toward her.

I pull it out. I hold it aloft, cuffs rattling at the movement. I think about the shift, the current, the riptide that flows around me. I remember how I brought Kyle with me to this timeline. I remember what Quint said: that maybe I could control the energy consciously, with practice.

The gun, I tell it. Not the cuffs. Bring the gun but not the cuffs.

The phone lands on a corner. It cracks. It bounces once, twice. It teeters on its edge and then starts to fall.

The shift curls itself around me but doesn't trigger yet.

I need a life-or-death situation. I heft the gun, take a step forward. I already know she won't hesitate.

The agent squeezes the trigger.

I'm gone before the phone hits the ground.

———

Silence comes first. The clatter of hail on the roof cuts to quiet. No thunder, no windows rattling in their frames from the bluster of the last timeline's storm. In the distance, the faint noise of city traffic blossoms.

Sight comes next. The fluorescents buzz steadily overhead, and a liquid golden daybreak leaks around the edges of the doors. I remember the last time I was here at dawn. A gray sunrise, pierced by skeletons of smoking framework.

Touch comes last. The gun is in my hand, its bumpy grip cool against my palms. The cuffs are gone.

So is Quint.

I push through the doors. I stand in the sunrise. I look to the south, to the swath of ash and char and barbed wire, and think about my ghost. I think about how far I've come to not kill him. I think about telling him I couldn't lose him. I think: *I'm afraid of the dark. All I have is you.*

Do it.

I tuck the gun into my waistband. And then I run for the ship.

Buildings blur. The sidewalk is cold and unyielding under my feet, and the cool fog of the coast seeps beneath my shirt. Halfway to the gate, a soldier spots me. His eyes narrow and he starts my way. Civilians aren't allowed here now.

But he's too far away and no one is stopping me today, not anymore. I crash through a side gate. The soldier fumbles, takes too long trying to reopen the gate behind me, and is soon out of sight.

I begin the long arc around the base.

The candy-bright signs start at the halfway point, where imposing cement buildings give way to debris. They clamor at me to turn back. RADIATION HAZARD. DANGER. NO TRESPASSING. I ignore them. I've gotten good at ignoring things during the last few weeks.

The space beside me is still empty, but I keep glancing at it anyway. It's like reaching for something just out of sight, grasping in the dark, waiting for your fingers to close around a familiar shape that's no longer there.

I reach the slit in the fence. The agents have put a temporary fix on it, but I kick through and wedge open a hole at the bottom that's barely wide enough for me to squeeze under. The edges of the fence scrape trenches across my shoulders, my back. Blood wells up. It trickles down my spine and soaks through my clothing. I'm grateful for the pain, the immediacy and simplicity of it, but it doesn't last long. Within seconds the blood slows and the wounds seal. The anxiety of this place doesn't vanish so easily, but it's buried beneath the desperation of what I have to do and it only takes me a minute or two to force myself to stand, to move forward.

The south end of the base is washed out in the dawn, colorless and quiet. I pass a fountain. Sheltered in the crook of two decimated buildings, it's scorched and cracked but not blown apart. The ash that once filled it is gone now, but I can still taste it. Bitter, thick, choking. Like I will never taste anything else ever again.

The shipyard looms. In the slanting light, one boat gleams a little more than the rest. When I draw nearer I see why. The chains, railings, almost every metal surface of the *McKay*, they're all bright as quicksilver. They glimmer until the sun's angle changes and then they fade into the background again, and the ship is nothing more than another broken down research vessel among a dozen of its counterparts. This is how Matthew has hid his Leratonium: the energy of millions of souls stretched thin over the metal of the agency's own ship.

I step out onto the plank. I walk over the algae-green water, and the deck creaks when I put my weight on it. There are no pigeons this time, no coffeepot, no feather. And no Matthew. I stand at the prow by myself, face to the sun, and wait.

Behind me, the plank creaks again.

"Will you remember?" I ask Matthew without turning around. "If it works, if the alternate timelines disappear and the world resets around you—will you remember the way it was?"

"My theories predict it," he answers. "Though I'd be the only one."

"And what will you do then?"

He steps up beside me, turns to face the sunrise. "Maybe I'll look you up," he says after a moment, and a strange sort of loneliness sweeps through his words. He gives me a sideways look and something in my expression makes him exhale. "No," he amends. "I won't."

The railing shines in front of me. It calls to me to touch it, the same way a canyon pulls you to fall when you stand at its edge. I keep my hands clenched tightly at my sides. "How does this work?" I ask him.

"You touch it," he says, nodding at the glimmering metal. "Anywhere. And channel his energy into it."

"I can't control it like that."

He raises an eyebrow, glancing down at the thin red lines around my wrists where the handcuffs used to be.

I grit my teeth. "And then what?"

"The computers below deck are already set. The wormhole will open as soon as it has enough energy. It sends my consciousness into the past version of myself, and then either I succeed and the world resets or I end up back here again and the space-time continuum disintegrates that much faster."

I take a breath. I turn. I step in close to Matthew, and the smell of mint and metal wraps us up and muffles the rest of the world. "Do you ever look at them?" I ask. "Before you kill them, do you talk to them? Did you talk to my dad? Did you tell him why?"

"I never look at them," he answers, and his eyes are the green sky before the storm.

"I hate you," I tell him. There's no turmoil, no bitter taste, only the truth.

His eyes turn curious. "But you don't hate Quint."

"He's not you."

"There's nothing else you can do for him, Camryn."

I take a breath. "There's this," I say.

I pull the gun out of my waistband. I aim it at him. I put my finger on the trigger.

He steps into the threat. The barrel of the gun lifts when it presses against his ribs. He tilts his head to look down at me, and our faces are barely a breath apart. "You'll shoot me," he says, and his voice is calm as a glassy sea. "You'll use up Quint and go back yourself. And then you'll still be a murderer, but I will be gone, and you'll remember him. You'll have everything you want."

I squeeze my eyes shut. The trigger feels foreign against my finger, too smooth, too easy. "That," I say, "is not everything I want."

"I told you there's no way out of this that doesn't end in death."

I open my eyes. His expression is oddly gentle. "And you're okay with it being your own?" I ask.

One side of his mouth quirks up in a quiet smile. "You can call it justice. I can live with that."

"But I can't," I tell him, and suddenly the gun feels exactly right in my hands—because he's wrong. There is another way out of this.

———

Leratonium: rushing through my veins. Radiation: still lingering all around the south end of the base. Electricity: neurons in my brain firing, synapses flickering like lightning in the night.

And a life-or-death situation to trigger my abilities.

I lift the gun. I turn it around. And I shoot myself in the stomach.

———

The pain is fuzzy and slow and red and burning, lava scorching a mountainside. For the second time today blood oozes between my fingers, but it's not quite as bright this time. Not an arterial bleed; a gut wound. Slower, because I need more time than Kyle had.

Quint's energy snakes around me, a waterfall of energy rushing toward the wound. This time I don't try to push it back. I redirect it instead, only a touch, enough to keep it flowing around the injury instead of healing it. The Leratonium in my veins tingles and rushes, searching for another way to keep me alive. A shift won't help. Only one thing will now.

———

The gun is still in my hand. I toss it overboard. It hits the green water and sinks, leaving the shadow of itself behind in the missing algae.

Matthew is shouting my name, reaching for me, eyes wide in alarm. I wrap my fingers around his, smearing blood across his knuckles. And then I wrap my other hand around the Leratonium railing and complete the circuit.

His fingers spasm in mine. His muscles go rigid and his spine arches, his head jerking back. He inhales, a gasping rattle that sounds like a drowning man. Something that feels like the wind is sweeping into my veins, tumbling past the tight currents of Quint's energy, tugged straight into the Leratonium on the other side like iron filings to a magnet.

And then it's gone.

Quint's energy noses after it, pulled out of the momentum of its spin by the call of the Leratonium, and I jerk away from the railing before it takes any of him.

Matthew's hand is still in mine. It's loose now, shaking but no longer spasming, and I go down onto my knees to keep ahold of it as he falls. I held his hand the last time he died, too.

His head cracks against the deck. His eyes are open and locked on mine, green like the storm, green like glass and the sea and betrayal, and I don't look away.

I could leave him here. I *want* to. How long would it take for his body to die, for his consciousness to leave it and follow his energy into the Leratonium? How long did it take the janitor? Fifty seconds, sixty seconds? And then his energy will be used up by the wormhole, and then he'll sink. Drift. Disappear. The same fate to which he's condemned millions.

But I know who I am now. And I'm still angry, so, so angry, but I think that might be okay—because I remember telling Quint it was your choices, not memories or the past or feelings, that determine who a person is.

Time to make mine.

I wrap his arm around my shoulder and pull us both to our feet.

The air above the prow gathers inward, pinching in on itself like wrinkled fabric. The light around it bends and warps. The wormhole. And next to it, exactly ten feet and three inches and an eternity from me: a see-through boy in a lab coat, reappearing from thin air.

He spots us, a bleeding girl and a dying boy staggering toward a crinkled patch of sky, and he understands. If I can get to the wormhole before Matthew's consciousness slips away, then I won't be a murderer. The boy I hate most will go to the past along with me, and he will help me fix everything, and then he will live. And Quint will be left behind. He won't die, he won't sink or drift or be forgotten, but he won't ever have existed either. It's all I can do for him.

Five more steps. Three. None. I'm face to face with my ghost.

———

Once, we were in a tunnel in the dark with only each other to talk to. Once we walked up a cliff, and I jumped, and he let me. Once we were enemies. And now we're standing at a wormhole with ten seconds to say goodbye and there's nothing left to say.

"I wanted to give you a happy ending," I manage at last. The pain wraps around the edges of my vision, blanketing the world in a gray haze.

Quint reaches out. He touches my cheek, smoke on skin. There's no warmth, no electricity, no vertigo, and now there never will be. Yet another loss to mourn. "You did," he answers, and then he gives me a grim smile because we both know that it's a lie and also the truth, and the best either of us can give each other now.

Five seconds left. I reach up, Matthew's hand in mine. I touch the wormhole. And the darkness sucks me away.

and panic crowding my thoughts as I search for a lab coat. Matthew is my best bet at stopping the explosion in time. If I can't find him, if he can't fix the experiment, if the wormhole spits us out back on that deck with nothing more than a new alternate timeline to show for it—then he'll be dead, and I'll be a murderer, and my family will be lost forever.

I bump into a soldier. I bounce off a car. I scramble onto its hood and climb on the roof, cup my hands around my mouth, scream his name.

People frown. A soldier turns and watches me, a band around her arm labeling her as military police. There's no sign of Matthew.

I slide off the car. The first time I met him, he was at the fountain. Maybe he's waiting there, or maybe he's already headed to the physics building. Or maybe he didn't get pulled through the wormhole at all and our mission is already doomed.

I sprint. I can't hear my shoes slapping against the pavement. I can't hear my breaths, though I know they're coming in loud, frantic gasps. I block everything out except *run* and *eight minutes* and *faster*.

I race into the courtyard. I skid to a stop at the lip of the fountain. Beyond the veil of spraying water, my memory superimposes an image: a boy sitting on the far edge, knees drawn up and back turned, holding his head.

I take a shuddering breath. I blink hard. I sidestep, but the vision stays the same.

It's not a memory. It's him. Matthew.

The fountain is too wide and I don't have time to run around it. I swing up and over. I splash through the shallow water, duck under the spray, grab Matthew by the collar and shove him to the sidewalk. I climb over after him.

He stays on the ground, hair falling over his glasses, staring up at me. Other people are staring, too. I grab a fistful of lab coat and yank him to his feet. I give him a shake—losing his energy on the ship must've put him into some kind of shock, because he's just blinking at me, confusion thick in his eyes.

He looks down at his chest. Then, slowly, he raises his fingers to touch my sleeve. "Camryn?" he says haltingly.

"Wake up, you bastard," I hiss. "We have seven minutes to fix your mistake."

His head lifts. His eyes change. He turns, and runs.

The physics building: half a mile across the base with no-nonsense architecture, wide glass doors, and heavy bronze handles. I reach out. I yank.

Boom. The earthquake rattles the building in its frame. The ground beneath us ripples like a sheet tugged tight, knocking me off balance, and I stagger into Matthew. His arms wrap around my ribcage, catching me. I shove him off, cursing, tears stinging my eyes—because it's not fair that he's warm and solid and alive, and the person I want him to be isn't.

The ground subsides. Two minutes left.

We sprint down the hall.

Two lefts and then a right. A long corridor. Room P-23. Matthew swipes his ID through the lock but it buzzes red. I shove him aside and pound on the door.

A stodgy man with a lab coat and a self-important expression pokes his head out. "Young lady," he says, "there is a very important—"

I punch him in the face.

He reels backward, holding his nose. Blood gushes out over his hands, and this time I allow myself to feel the regret without being paralyzed by it, because this is too important and too necessary and the damage is minor anyway. He shouts and gurgles, but I push past him, heedless, bowling through the scientists to clear a path for Matthew. He barrels through after me, intent on a row of computers at the front of the room. He tosses aside a chair, puts his hands on a keyboard—and then stops.

There's a hand on my shoulder, and someone has a crushing grip on my arm. Someone else is shouting the name *Kingfisher,* and no one is getting violent yet because they know who my mother is, but I can only hold them back for another second. "Do it!" I shout.

He hesitates, frozen. Then a revelation washes over his face and he plunges a hand into his pocket. A quicksilver-gray rock falls out with a dull *thunk.* A piece of paper flutters: the experiment's corrected settings. He punches in the numbers and then stops again, staring at the screen.

I shove a middle-aged woman in a lab coat away, but someone is shouting for MPs and bodies are surrounding me, dragging me toward the door, drowning me. People are squeezing past and heading for Matthew.

He looks up. He meets my eyes. He lifts the paper. It's a series of seven numbers, the new calibrations for the electrical trigger. "I never wrote down the last digit," Matthew shouts, desperation tearing at his words.

Overhead the skylight darkens, throwing rushing shadows across the rows of computers. Birds spiral toward the sun. Our time in the past is almost up.

The moment quiets. A memory reaches out, tucks itself around me: a boy in an ambulance, trying to remember his name. *I think it might have something to do with the number five,* he'd said. *That was the first thing I thought about when I came to.*

"Five!" I shout, and then someone clamps a hand around my mouth and drags me back toward the door and I can't see Matthew, I can't see the computer, all I can see are the swirling birds and the darkened sky and our time ticking to an end.

I'm a leaf in a current of bodies. The MPs sweep me out of the room, down the corridor. I turn my head: birds darting past the windows, a flurry of feathers and light. Through the MPs I catch a glimpse of lab coat and blond hair. Matthew's caught in the current too.

I shut my eyes and take a breath. I feel the countdown in my bones. The earthquake, the birds, the end of the world. Forty seconds left.

The MPs shove me in a room, not bothering to turn on the lights before they lock the door and head back toward the experiment to check the damage. There's one window in here, high and tiny and barred, but its screen is open. I scoop up a chair and stand on it and turn my face to the sky. Feathers. Shadows. Chaos.

A noise at my back. They put someone else in here with me. And I know it's Matthew Lerato, bomber, blackmailer, murderer, but I can't help turning around anyway—because if this is the end of my world then I don't want to be alone, and he has the face of my ghost.

But he's not looking at me. He's sitting with his back to the door, curled around a phone, jabbing at its screen with shaking fingers. He hits one last button and then lays the phone on the ground, splaying a hand atop it. His head is bowed and his hair is over his eyes and I can't see his face, and I need to see his face.

"Quint," I say, which is the wrong name, but I can't say anything else.

He looks up. His eyes are bright and haunted and he shakes his head, and suddenly I don't want to look at him after all. My eyes fall to his phone.

"I told them," he says, taking his hand away from it.

My gaze lifts again. "What? Who?"

He scrubs a hand through his hair, covers his eyes. "Everyone," he says, his voice muffled. "I told everyone everything. I just released my entire database of Leratonium research to the public domain. Not the specifics, not the formula, but the results. The experiments. What the agency did. What I did to stop them. What happened, what I'd theorized *could* happen. Everything."

I stare at him. I step down from the chair. My mind tilts slowly, an unbalanced scale.

Matthew was afraid. Everything he did was to run from that fear, to avoid living with his mistakes. Even at the end, when he wanted me to shoot him—even that was his way of running, his final way of not having to live with what he's done.

And now, voluntarily, moments before he might die without anyone ever having to know his wrongs, he's told the world everything.

I remember when he saw me at the fountain. The confusion in his eyes, the way it shifted into a sort of wonder when he touched my sleeve. The way he said my name.

An impossible hope twists deep into me.

I cross the room. I kneel in front of him. "Quint," I say again, shaping the word like it's a breakable thing.

He looks up at me. "Yes," he says, but it comes out uncertain. And then, more firmly: "No."

The hope curls in on itself. I don't say anything.

He swallows once, twice, lining up the words in his head before he says them. "You sent Matthew's consciousness and your own through the wormhole."

I nod. I wait.

"But your consciousness was tied to Quint's, so he got sent through too," he says, and my heart thumps hard, but he shakes his head. "Two versions of Matthew Lerato got pulled to the past. But there was only one body here for him. We got...mixed back together, into the same person again." He meets my gaze, raw and miserable. "Camryn, I'm *him*."

And suddenly those green eyes are wrong. That expression is wrong. His words are *wrong*, they're horrific and cruel and impossible, because if I let them be true then this is even worse than Quint being gone altogether. Everything I've done, the price we both paid, it's only brought him to the one thing he was trying hardest to escape.

My breath stalls. My hands drop from his. I stand up and pull away—

And then stop.

His phone is still glowing at my feet. The Wi-Fi-based upload indicator is blinking at one-hundred-percent. I bend down, scoop it up, cup it in my hands. I look up at the boy who is both Matthew and Quint and then, slowly, a hypothesis forms. It's murky and shadowed, but I can see the outline of an answer, and it gleams with something like hope.

I kneel back down. "What did my father say when you killed him?" I ask softly.

He covers his face again. "Don't," he chokes out.

Pain spirals tight inside me. I press him anyway, because I have to test my hypothesis. "That's what he said, or that's what you're saying now?"

He drops his hands, which are still shaking. He looks up at me. "He…was at work. It caught him by surprise. He didn't have time to say anything."

"You have Matthew's memories."

He squeezes his eyes shut and nods.

I wrap my fingers around the phone. A weight is crushing

my chest and there's a part of me that wants to run from this conversation, but I can't abandon it now, not until I know. "When we were in the janitor's closet, me and Quint, you told me you used to hate me. What did you say was the reason?"

"You had memories and a body and a family, and all I had was you."

"And what did I say?"

He opens his eyes. He doesn't reply.

"That memories don't make a person," I answer. "That choices do. And," I say, holding out his phone between us, barely daring to breathe, "this doesn't look like Matthew's choice to me."

He swallows. He stretches out a hand and lifts the phone away, careful not to touch me. He stares at the screen. "But I'm him," he says, though the words are softer now and they rise at the end like he's asking a question.

The hope is spreading and twisting, but I force myself to wait. To stay where I am, to keeping talking, to see if the theory takes root. "When I found you at the fountain a few minutes ago, you were confused."

He's still looking at the phone. "Two minds in one body. It was...a struggle."

"And who won?"

He raises his head. He watches me.

"You told me to do it, back at the warehouse. To use you

up," I say. "You faced your fears, and Matthew never could, not even at the end. Maybe that made you stronger than him. And now you're the one making the decisions, and all that's left of him are memories."

He tests the idea. He weighs it, balances it, totals it up, and considers the sum. His expression turns hopeful instead of horrified.

Then his gaze focuses over my shoulder. A smile spreads across his face and my heart flops over in my chest, because he's never looked more like Quint. I turn around to follow his gaze; he's looking at the window. A fat pigeon is strutting across the sill, fluffing its wings. It pecks at the bricks, finds nothing of interest, and flaps off to a nearby tree with a disgruntled coo.

It leaves behind a feather.

I stand on tiptoe and stretch my fingers between the bars to reach it. It's long, ash gray, light as hope in my hand.

I think it means redemption.

Quint checks his watch and looks back at me, his expression brilliant as the sun. "Cam, it's been two minutes. It didn't happen."

It didn't happen. The end of my world has ticked past, just another unremarkable second, and we're still here. Somewhere on the base, my mother is alive. Somewhere in the city, my dad and brother are well and whole. My future is intact, reset. It's anything I want it to be, anything I can make it.

Quint gets up. He stands next to me to look out the window, and if I close my eyes I can imagine it's still my old ghost standing there, insubstantial but certain, tied to me like he's always been.

I keep my eyes open.

The feather tickles my palm. Quint is watching me. His smile is gone now, and a question has replaced it.

I hold out my hand. I offer him the feather, and answer it.

EPILOGUE

WHEN QUINT ARRIVES, I'M PERCHED at the top of the subway stairs, bare feet tucked beneath me, the tattered hem of my prom dress pooled on the steps. It's a few minutes past midnight, and a trickle of late-night passengers step around me on their way to the subway. Beyond the barred windows of the train station, the late spring moon is rising.

My back is to the door that Quint comes through, but I feel the moment he spots me. The change in the air is like a current switching on; the night goes from fuzzy and lethargic to something that feels like holding your breath in the space of half a second.

He pauses, watching from the doorway. I don't say

anything. After a long moment, he crosses the wide open space and moves toward me, steps painfully slow.

He sits at my side, careful to leave six inches between us. "Hi," he says. His gaze slips in my direction. Three weeks of confinement at the Washington base have left their stamp on his expression—uncertain, vulnerable, a little bit haunted.

Or maybe it's just me.

I'm holding a cream soda in each hand. I toss him one and he catches it, turning the glass bottle over and examining it like it might contain some kind of secret message. "We're celebrating," I inform him.

He arches a brow. "My graduation to house arrest?" He shifts after he says it, self-conscious, and I catch a glimpse of the black tracker around his ankle. The agency was forced to release him yesterday by order of the Army higher-ups who are investigating the experiment, but he's still only allowed to go a few miles from his new apartment. Now that he's a military whistle-blower, his life will probably never be easy again. I don't think he regrets it, though. I think that, finally, Quint is at peace with his choices.

"No," I answer. "I decided to accept my scholarship at State. Pre-med degree, here I come." I clink my bottle against his and down a gulp. Still uncertain, he follows suit. "Also," I continue, "the panic disorder treatment I'm doing means I have to ride this damn subway for another half hour while tolerating the anxiety, and I need the fortification. Kyle wouldn't buy me anything stronger, so this'll have to do."

Quint presses his lips together against a smile and glances over his shoulder at my family. Mom waves from her spot in front of the ticket booth, her new pearl earrings glittering in the fluorescent light.

She laughed last week when she opened the gift-wrapped jewelry box. It had taken me a while to find a pair that looked exactly like the ones she'd given up for me when I was thirteen, and she recognized them immediately.

She put the earrings on with a rueful smile. "That awful manager hurt you, and I wanted to make you feel better. And I kind of wanted you to think I was a badass too," she admitted.

I tucked her chestnut hair behind her ears. "You're my badass," I told her, and we squeezed the life out of each other in the mushiest hug ever.

Next to Mom at the ticket booth, Dad gives an exagger-ated yawn and a thumbs-up. Kyle is sitting in a chair next to them, clad in his agency uniform, feet propped up on the ticket booth and hands behind his head like he doesn't care how I'm doing—but every time I return to this stop I spot him cracking open one eye to make sure the panic isn't drag-ging me under.

It is, but I'm letting it, and the result is kind of like realizing I can breathe underwater—accepting the fear instead of running and hiding and denying lets me prove to myself that I can handle it, and because of that fragile newfound confidence, the panic hasn't been escalating to nearly the levels it used to. I still hate it, and I still feel helpless a lot, but there's a light at the end of the tunnel now. Literally, in this case.

Quint is fiddling with his bottle and not looking at me. "Your mom said you wanted me here," he says, almost like it's a question.

He has good reason to wonder at my motives. Mom went to visit him a couple times over the last few weeks, but I never accompanied her. I needed time to figure out how I felt. When you've been through so much with someone, sometimes it's hard to separate the experience from the person. It's even harder when that person was actually two people, and when one of them was a mass murderer.

"Yep," I say, but don't elaborate because I'm still getting the words I want to say right in my head.

He glances over, taking in my tattered, paintball-splotched strapless dress. "How are you not cold?" he asks.

"Oh, I'm freezing. But two rides back I accidentally left my very fancy and expensive wrap on my seat, and some lucky subway rider has probably snatched it."

He shrugs out of his hoodie—gray, soft, a little bit worn around the edges—and drops it over my head. "Should I even ask what happened to your shoes?" he wonders, but I can't answer for a moment, because the hoodie is warm and enveloping and it smells like...

Pine.

He notices my expression. "What?"

I clear my throat. "It smells," I say, and then can't continue.

He blinks. "I swear I washed it yesterday," he says, and I swallow a laugh.

"No," I try again. "It smells like pine. Not like mint and metal."

He processes this statement, then looks away. The silence is heavier than before.

I return my gaze to the steps. "I lost one shoe at the stop on Maple ten minutes back," I tell him. "Tripped over a curb and the whole heel came right off. I figured I might as well lose the other one, too. I tried to tell Mom I'd rather just wear my Converse and jeans to the dance earlier. Can't go home to get them now, though, not without ruining my exposure exercise." I wave a hand at the subway below.

"Oh," he says, still looking at my dress. "Was it...prom night, earlier?" I hear the question behind the words—he wants to know if I had a date, but he's not sure it's his right to ask.

"Yeah. I was supposed to go stag, but I ended up ditching it anyway. Kyle's home this weekend, so I dragged him out to play some paintball instead, and then I realized what today was."

"Three weeks," he says.

Three weeks since the explosion that didn't happen. Three weeks that we experienced twice—once with him tied to me, and once after we reset the space-time continuum. Tomorrow is the first day I haven't already lived.

I burrow a little deeper into his hoodie. "It felt right, being here. Doing this part of the treatment tonight."

He's turning the bottle over and over in his hands, expression tight as he stares down the steps. It was only a few feet from here that he told me I'd end up killing my brother just like I'd killed my mother. And it was only a few yards in the opposite direction that another version of him planted a bomb that leveled a city block, and changed the course of my life forever.

"I told your mom everything," he says suddenly, and the words are low and urgent, tripping over each other like he's not sure how long I'll listen. "I wrote it all down for the court case she's helping with, for the people in Washington who are thinking about shutting the agency down. They're planning an initiative to make sure Leratonium never gets misused again."

"She told me," I reply, but he doesn't seem to hear.

"I destroyed all my original research, everything I didn't

release to the public. I made sure the agency couldn't access any of the calibrations, the formula. And I never answered their questions. None of them."

I lift my bottle of cream soda and take a deep gulp because I need fortification for this moment too, and then I turn to Quint. "Shut up," I tell him. "There's something I want to say to you."

He blinks. In his hands, the bottle stills. Then before I can go on, he drops one hand in his pocket, pulls something out, and, after a moment's hesitation, offers it to me.

A pigeon feather. It's slightly crinkled, but beyond a few bent barbs it looks exactly like it did the day I gave it to him.

The words I'd finally figured out die without reaching my lips, because they weren't right anyway. Only one thing can be, for this moment—with the world narrowed to a split second, to a choice, to a feather in the hand of a boy who was once my hallucination and then my ally and then, against all logic, the person I fell for.

I lean over. I look at him—green eyes bright, hesitant, questioning—and kiss him.

Electricity. Vertigo. I'm standing at the top of a theme park zip line, stepping out over the empty air.

He lifts a hand and touches my cheek. His fingertips are warm and solid and, when the kiss ends, he leans his forehead against mine and inhales like it's the first breath he's ever taken.

"If you break her heart, I'll kill you," Kyle calls lazily, and the moment is over.

I lean away, smothering a grin. "Careful," I call over my shoulder. "You're in danger of looking affectionate."

I look back at Quint, who's now sitting very still and staring at me. I wait to see what he'll say. Whether he'll kiss me again.

But he swallows and touches his now-crooked glasses, searching for words. "I...I still have Matthew's memories."

My grin fades. "I know."

"It's confusing. I want to, God, I want to, but I don't know if I can—if we can—" He spreads his hands, helpless.

"I know," I say, because I do. It's why I never visited him, why I could never bear to call or write. He's the boy I fell for, but he also has all the memories of the boy I hate most. And yes, it's hard and terrible and confusing—but in some strange way, it also feels right. Because don't we all have to live with the shards of ourselves? With all those bits of our souls that we hate, all the puzzle pieces we'd rather hide from?

I take a breath, searching for a way to tell Quint how I feel about everything that's happened between us, the conclusions I've come to. "I killed him," I say at last.

He looks up sharply.

"Matthew," I go on. "I stole his soul and watched him

fall. And yeah, I picked him back up again, I did my part to save him—but all my actions were based on guesses, on best-case scenarios, and it could've gone the other way just as easily. And at the end of the day, he's gone anyway. What does that make me?"

Quint frowns. He reaches out, hesitates, and then tucks a strand of hair behind my ear. "Complicated," he says softly. "But a good person anyway."

I put my hand over his, trapping it. "Yeah," I say. "Same as you."

His smile is slow but unguarded, crinkled at the corners, lighting him up from the inside. "And…you're okay with complicated?"

"I'm okay with you. When you're not being a jackass and/or a manipulative bastard."

He snorts. "I can't make any promises."

"Shut up," I order, and kiss him again.

AUTHOR'S NOTE

ALTHOUGH THIS BOOK IS a work of fiction, the anxiety Camryn deals with is a very real experience for many teens. If her struggle resonates with you, please know that you are not alone.

For help with panic disorder or any other form of anxiety, you can visit calmclinic.com. Between the hours of 6–10 p.m. Pacific Time, teenagers can also call Teen Line at (800) TLC-TEEN ([800] 852-8336) to talk to teen volunteer listeners trained to provide support for those dealing with anxiety, depression, bullying, and a wide range of other issues.

ACKNOWLEDGMENTS

T HE MAKING OF THIS BOOK was a long, round-
about, and exhausting/exhilarating process, and there
were so many people who helped turn it into an actual
Book-Shaped Thing. Some of them helped me improve
my story through critique, some advocated it to their connections in the publishing industry, and some I cheerfully
conned into babysitting for me so I could get some writing
done (sorry, hon). I owe so much to all of them.

First and foremost, I have to thank my agent, Kira
Watson, who was the best possible champion *Afterimage*
could've had and one of the first people to truly believe in it.
I promise I'll name a villain after you someday!

Thanks to my awesome editor, Lauren Knowles, who

caught all of the wibbly-wobbly timey-wimey mistakes left over from when this story's timelines were even more complicated, and the team at Page Street Publishing, especially Rosie Stewart, badass designer extraordinare! I'm so thrilled I got to partner with you all in the making of this book. I also want to give a shout-out to Ashley Hearn, who helped introduce *Afterimage* to Lauren Knowles, and who is a pretty stellar editor herself.

Thanks to my critique partners: Casey Lyall, Chelsea Bobulski, and Alicia Jasinski. Buy their books, these ladies are seriously amazing writers! Thanks also to the incredibly generous authors who put in a good word for me while *Afterimage* was out on submission: Wade Albert White, Jennifer Park, and N.K. Traver. And an extra big helping of thanks to Brenda Drake, author and creator of the Pitch Wars contest, which changed my life five years ago when I first started seriously writing and set me on the path to where I am today.

This story got read by so many people over the last few years. Without their thoughtful critique and constructive criticism, *Afterimage* would be a much shabbier version of itself. There were a few amazing ladies in particular whose notes were instrumental in the development and revision of *Afterimage*: Lydia Sharp, Jennifer Hawkins (my medical expert!), and Serene Hakim.

A big thank you to Kate Brauning, whose editorial

mentorship meant the world to me and vastly improved my writing and revising skills as well as my editorial ones.

Thank you to my real-life friends, who help keep me surprisingly sane on a daily basis: Britton, Becky, Janette, Lisa, and Shawna.

While brainstorming the science-y-ness of this story, one book in particular came in very handy: *Physics of the Impossible* by Michio Kaku. I also have to give credit to Neil deGrasse Tyson's *Cosmos: A Spacetime Odyssey*, a thoroughly fantastic show that gave me the first nugget of an idea for the concept that would become *Afterimage*. And while we're at it, let's have a huge, geektastic shout-out to some of the awesome TV shows and movies (some of which I totally Easter-egged in this book) that inspired part of this story's tone and themes: *Doctor Who* (which is only the best TV show ever, and in case you're wondering, I'm an 11th-Doctor girl), *Avatar: The Last Airbender*, Marvel's *Doctor Strange* and *Captain America* movies, *Pacific Rim*, *Harry Potter*, BBC's *Sherlock, Stargate: Atlantis, Mythbusters, Star Wars*, and *Pushing Daisies*.

When I was researching the panic disorder element of this book, *The Panic Attacks Workbook* by Dr. David Carbonell was hugely helpful. I want to thank Andrea as well—her advice and support brought me out of a dark time with my own anxiety, and she provided valuable feedback for elements of this story.

I also want to thank my favorite author, who has had a huge impact on my writing, as well as on how much time I spend not doing the dishes while re-reading her books: Megan Whalen Turner, author of the immeasurably amazing *Queen's Thief* series.

And of course, I have to thank my family. My husband Caleb distracted our adorable, small daughter for countless hours while I hid in various locations trying to write and revise this book (Dear Caleb: If you would just put in a lock for my office door that our child can't pick with her tiny but surprisingly dexterous fingers, this would all be much easier), plus he lent me his scientist's brain whenever I needed it for world-building questions. Thanks to my brother Nathan. Kyle is totally not based on you, just in case you were wondering. Thanks to my parents, who will finally be allowed to read this book now that it's published and they can't convince me to take all the cursing out. And thanks to Steve and Ronda, who have always supported me.

Even though she can't read yet, I want to thank my daughter, who is my whole heart and all my inspiration. May I someday measure up to the woman I am in your eyes.

Lastly, thanks to the God Who put this passion for stories inside me. Without You, none of this would be possible.

ABOUT
THE AUTHOR

 **N**AOMI HUGHES GREW UP ALL over the U.S. before finally settling in the Midwest, a place she loves even though it tries to murder her with tornadoes every spring. She writes quirky young adult fiction full-time and works as a freelance editor. In her free time she likes to knit, travel with her husband and daughter, and geek out over British TV and Marvel superheroes.